$\mathcal{W}$hat the critics are saying...

ജ

4 Stars "Bast has written a tantalizing treat in which two men find ultimate pleasure in satisfying the needs of one woman. The ending is exciting and tense." ~ *Romantic Times BOOKclub*

"Anya Bast strikes again! A Changes of Season is a great erotic story that will heat up the coldest of winter nights. ... I recommend that readers pick up A Change of Season, the story is truly wonderful." ~ *Euro Reviews*

"Anya Bast's A Change of Season is a gripping story of life-saving love and passion, wild and tame at the same time, both scary and wonderful, and so very erotic. Dain is a tortured man and it is Moira's love that brings him back from the brink of despair and self-loathing.... with a very good mystery thrown in, you are in for a wonderfully lustful and unbridled read." ~ *Historical Romance Club*

"This is a book with such a compelling and tortured lead and a woman so in love with him she's willing to accept whatever she can while it's available that you will find your self submerged in their explosive emotions.... Definitely a gripping fantasy that will capture and stimulate readers with characters and a plot they can sink their teeth into." ~ *Enchanted in Romance*

Anya Bast

A Change of Season

ELLORA'S CAVE
ROMANTICA PUBLISHING

An Ellora's Cave Romantica Publication

www.ellorascave.com

A Change of Season

ISBN #1419953834
ALL RIGHTS RESERVED.
A Change of Season Copyright © 2005 Anya Bast
Edited by Biana St. James
Cover art by Syneca

Electronic book Publication August 2005
Trade paperback Publication May 2006

Excerpt from *And Lady Makes Three* Copyright © Anya Bast,
Nikki Soarde, Ashley Ladd, 2005

Excerpt from *Ellora's Cavemen: Dreams of the Oasis I* Copyright ©
2006

Excerpt from *Nuworld: Thicker than Water* Copyright © Lorie O'
Clare, 2006

Warning:

The following material contains graphic sexual content meant for mature readers. This story has been rated E–rotic by a minimum of three independent reviewers.

Ellora's Cave Publishing offers three levels of Romantica™ reading entertainment: S (S-ensuous), E (E-rotic), and X (X-treme).

S-*ensuous* love scenes are explicit and leave nothing to the imagination.

E-*rotic* love scenes are explicit, leave nothing to the imagination, and are high in volume per the overall word count. In addition, some E-rated titles might contain fantasy material that some readers find objectionable, such as bondage, submission, same sex encounters, forced seductions, and so forth. E-rated titles are the most graphic titles we carry; it is common, for instance, for an author to use words such as "fucking", "cock", "pussy", and such within their work of literature.

X-*treme* titles differ from E-rated titles only in plot premise and storyline execution. Unlike E-rated titles, stories designated with the letter X tend to contain controversial subject matter not for the faint of heart.

Also by Anya Bast

ຂ

And Lady Makes Three *(anthology)*
Blood of an Angel
Blood of the Raven
Blood of the Rose
Ordinary Charm
Seasons of Pleasure: Autumn Pleasures: The Union
Seasons of Pleasure: Spring Pleasures: The Transformation
Seasons of Pleasure: Summer Pleasures: The Capture
Seasons of Pleasure: Winter Pleasures: The Training
Water Crystal

About the Author

ຂ

Anya Bast writes erotic fantasy and paranormal romance. Primarily, she writes happily-ever-afters with lots of steamy sex. After all, how can you have a happily-ever-after WITHOUT lots of sex?

Anya welcomes mail from readers. You can write to her c/o Ellora's Cave Publishing at 1056 Home Avenue, Akron, OH 44310-3502.

A Change of Season

ജ

Dedication

ಳು

Dedicated with much affection to Anni, Renee and Patti,
who wanted Indian Summer.

Preface

From A Brief History of New Ecasian Civilization, by Thomas ki Haeffen.

&

As all textbooks will tell you, Ecasia was split apart by a war in the year 602 and separated into two countries, Sudhra and Nordan. This separation occurred primarily because of a curse set down by the Goddess Ariane in retribution for the ill-use of her female children by her male children. Ariane deemed that the seed of the males would not take root but rarely and thus begun the long struggle for the survival of both the Nordanese and Sudhraians.

Those in Sudhra renounced the Goddess and chose to worship the God Anot, principally. Those in Nordan chose to try and appease the Goddess and worshiped her primarily, treating their women with love and respect in an effort to cause the Goddess to lift her curse.

In the year 1163, a war broke out between the two countries, instigated by Sudhra, but won by Nordan. This war, though short, was one of the most important events in Ecasian history. It reunited the two halves of a whole and ended the Goddess' curse through an incident now referred to as The Miracle, an event explored in depth in the chapter entitled Lord Gregor and the Lady Anaisse. (See page 374.)

Thus the united country of New Ecasia was born. It was first comprised of the territories of Nordan and Sudhra, but in the year 1165, under the governance of Lord Rue d'Ange and Lady Lilane, the territory of Aeoli was formed. Aeoli is the stronghold of the Aviat and exists in the far northern reaches of Nordan. Under the direction of Lady Anaisse and

Lord Gregor, one other small territory was formed called the Port of Paradise. The tiny territory of the Port of Paradise exists on the border of Sudhra and Nordan and remains to this day a neutral place of democratic governance for the country of New Ecasia.

Not only did the Goddess lift her curse, she also granted a special gift to those first children conceived and born at the conclusion of the war. Not all, but most postwar children were born with varying levels of magick that have continued down their bloodlines to this very day. They are called the Blessed Ones, or in some parts of the territory of Sudhra, the Cursed Ones.

After the Sudhraian–Nordanese war and the lifting of the Goddess' curse, there was a period of peace in New Ecasia's history. It is referred to as The One Hundred Year Peace.

Lord Gregor of Nordan and his wife Lady Anaisse of Sudhra were primarily honored for uniting the two warring lands, ending the long-lived curse of the Goddess Ariane on the men, and bringing that time of peace and plenty. Others are cited in the history books as having a hand. Lord Marken and Lord Talyn and their wives, Sienne and Raven, had roles to play. Lord Rue and his wife, Lilane, were the ones who risked a trip into enemy territory and a dangerous ruse to aid Nordan in their campaign.

But the dogs of war are always panting and humans are slow to learn life's lessons. Eventually, war came once again to the united land of New Ecasia when General Morgan organized New Ecasia's army into overthrowing the democratic system of rule in the Port of Paradise and taking it over. General Morgan soon became Emperor Morgan as he conquered and dragged the neighboring lands under his cold iron-fisted rule.

And New Ecasia suffered once more.

But you can only subjugate and enslave people to a point. Once you cross the line and their faces are pushed into the mud one too many times, their farms and homes are taxed once too often, their stomachs rumble with hunger while the ruling class dine on truffles and fatten themselves on rich cheese and wine one night too many...revolution breaks out.

In the year 1280 the revolution began. It shredded the country from the southern reaches of Sudhra to the northernmost peaks of the Aeoli Mountains. The war ended in 1283 with the dictator Morgan vanquished and the democratic system of New Ecasia once again in place in the Port of Paradise.

Chapter One
New Ecasia, Nordan territory — the year 1288

ॐ

The cup slipped from Moira's fingers and crashed to the wooden floor of her home. Pain speared through her mind, bringing her to her knees. She braced her hands on her thighs and concentrated on the broken cup, breathing in through her nose and out her mouth. Her head felt broken, too, as though her mind had split like the cup and the shards grated against each other in an effort to put itself back together. Nausea welled up and she swallowed hard in an effort to force it away.

The episodes got worse with every passing day. She clenched her fists, realizing there may be no way to stave them off before they consumed her. She'd thought the last herbal concoction she'd made would suppress the image flashes, but they obviously hadn't helped in the least.

The pain faded along with the last lingering picture in her mind's eye. With a growing sense of dread, she gathered up the broken pieces of the cup and stood. Moira laid them on her table and sank down into one of the rough-hewn chairs that flanked it. The fire in the hearth glowed merrily — in direct contrast to her emotions — and chased away the insidious late autumn cold that slipped under the crack of her cottage door and through the edges of her shuttered windows.

Her bed stood in the corner, made up with a multicolored quilt and several pillows that villagers had traded her for her herbal remedies and counseling. Dried herbs hung from the wooden rafters above her head.

Her house was not well appointed or large, but it was snug, warm and safe and she didn't want to leave it, especially not in obedience to the compulsion that so relentlessly pursued her these days.

This Lord Cyric. Goddess protect her. Deep dread accompanied the mere whisper of his name on her lips or the image of his face that seemed burned into her mind's eye. His eyes were gray as the cloud-filled night sky and bereft of soul. The set of his jaw, the thin press of his lips, his razor-sharp chin. All of his features she saw with her every breath and would give anything to banish them.

She shivered in revulsion. Why did perceptions of the man fill her mind so often these days, accompanied by the sharp pains through her temple that could bring her to her knees? The Powers, the Goddess Ariane and the God Anot, had been screaming at her to leave the cottage and travel, likely toward this repulsive stranger. The more she resisted, the stronger the compulsion grew. This man had an aura of evil. Why would The Powers want to endanger her?

It had to be a mistake, she reasoned.

Moira stood, took her gray woolen coat from its peg by the door and drew it over her shoulders, then picked up the bucket that stood beneath it on the floor. Better to put his image from her mind. Better to go on about her life as though these attacks did not plague her, as though The Powers were not commanding her to seek out a man whose very name felt synonymous with death and destruction.

She needed water to wash with, and to cook. She had wood to gather and remedies to brew. It was past time she got on with her day. The wind snatched her breath away as she left her cottage. It blew the door shut behind her with a violent crash. Early morning gloom coated the forest in murky hues and the boughs of the trees creaked in the chill wind.

Moira was born of a family line connected to the Lady Sienne and Lord Marken, and as a direct descendent of their firstborn child, Galen, she'd inherited a healthy dose of magick. It had been the Goddess Ariane's gift to the first born of New Ecasia when she'd lifted the curse.

She'd moved out to the forest after the latent magick within her had manifested itself. Her powers of empathy had grown so great that living close to others had been noisy and emotionally excruciating.

At least in this part of the territory of Nordan people accepted her magick. In some regions of Sudhraian Territory, deep in the southern part of New Ecasia, the magicked ones were not considered blessed, but cursed. Aye, it'd been meant as a blessing, a gift, but in some of the still backward parts of the former country of Sudhra, magick was considered the mark of evil.

She had more control over her abilities now, but had grown used to living in solitude. Out in the forest, away from most people, it was quiet and peaceful. Those who valued her ability to read into their present and their past, and counsel them on what she saw would travel out to see her on a regular basis. She'd made a decent living trading on her skill so far. Moira kept her visits to the village to a minimum, only going when she needed supplies. Her family and friends, the ones who were not magick-averse, traveled to see her occasionally. If sometimes she was a little lonely, well, so be it. Everything had its cost.

She walked down the path to her well. Twigs cracked under her boots and the wind whipped her skirts around her legs and her hair into her face. She tied her bucket to the rope and drew water. Her muscles protested the movement and she rested the bucket on the stone rim of the well, staring at the rippling reflections in the surface of the water. For a moment, they mesmerized her with the shimmering in the waning light. Abruptly, they formed an image.

Blinding pain burst through her head and she fell backward with a cry. This time it was not Lord Cyric's visage that filled her mind, but another man's face. She didn't recognize the rough-hewn features and eyes of pale, otherworldly shade of blue. However she well recognized the name that breathed through her mind. Though she'd never laid physical eyes on him, she knew that name and the reputation of the one who bore it. Lord Dain d'Ange. But she didn't want to be anywhere near Lord Dain, the winged devourer of women. No woman in her right mind would.

Lord Dain.

Aye. Everyone knew about the mad Lord of Aeoli, a man also descended from the first of the magicked ones. He was an Aviat, from Lord Rue and Lady Lilane's line. Even witch-hermits like her had heard the stories about that one.

Oh, what dangerous and tangled web of fate had the Goddess woven around her now?

His face reasserted itself in her mind with a fresh and vicious stab of pain. Blessedly, she slipped into darkness.

* * * * *

Dain knelt in the dry, rocky soil of what had once been his wife's garden and pulled a rogue Narrdine blossom from the soil. He stood and glanced around at the weed-overgrown area. Andreea had loved her garden when she'd been alive. She'd had such a way with the plants and flowers that she and the gardeners had barely been able to keep the garden tamed because it had bloomed so profusely.

But like everything else, the garden had died when Andreea had died. The summer had turned to autumn and then the harsh, cold bleakness of Aeolian wintertime had set in. The flowers had disappeared.

So had the gardeners and the keep's servants, the stable hands and the bulk of his men. So had most of his tenant farmers and retainers. Dain had sent most of them away, driven the rest of them from the castle. A few of the more stubborn remained yet.

And the magick. The magick that ran through his veins was an ever-present companion, reminding him of his failure, his lack of control. He dropped the blossom to the ground and walked away.

Dain passed under the crumbling stone archway separating the garden from the courtyard. The barking of his two dogs barely reached in to tickle his consciousness, he was so deep in thought, immersed in memory.

"My lord."

Dain looked up to see William watching him from the center of the courtyard. The middle-aged jack-of-all-trades scratched the top of his balding head. "Got a visitor at the gate." He motioned toward the barbican.

"A visitor?" There hadn't been a soul who'd approached Aeodan Keep voluntarily for more than a year and a half. There weren't any who dared.

"Aye. A young woman come in from the Nordanese countryside by the looks of her clothing. She's asking for you."

Dain stood staring at William for a moment, dumbfounded.

"Want me to run her off, my lord?"

Dain pursed his lips. He was sufficiently intrigued to do it himself. "No. I'll get her gone."

Pebbles and grit crunched under his boots as he walked toward the barbican. He could see that William had left the heavy wooden door open, though the portcullis was still down. A thin, small figure stood huddled by the gate, dressed in the drab gray wrappings of a commoner. A saddled gray mare stood near her, cleaning the gravel road of a few stubborn weeds.

Blix and Athna, his large black dogs, trotted up to flank him as he approached the gate. Curiously, they did not bark or growl, as they always did with strangers. Athna gave a little whine when they approached the woman and settled down at his feet. Blix sat on his opposite side, his ears forward and lithe body alert.

He appraised the woman before he addressed her. An old, ratty scarf wrapped her head, concealing her hair, though a few blood-red strands had freed themselves to fall around her heart-shaped, pale face. Dark smudges marred the skin beneath dark green eyes. Eyes that watched him now with no small measure of trepidation. Her lips were parted and a streak of dirt marked one of her cheeks. She looked perhaps about five years or so younger than himself. Her reddened and chapped fingers gripped the bars of the portcullis.

"What do you want?" he growled at her. "We've no work here and we give out no charity."

"I only beg an interview, my lord. A few hours if you can spare them."

"What for?"

She shifted in apparent uneasiness. "It is a delicate matter, my lord, and one that requires a large amount of careful explanation. Suffice it to say that I require a dialogue." Her speech took him aback. She did not speak like a commoner, but as a highborn. Whoever she was, she was educated. "What demon from the Underworld could compel you to wish to spend time with me, girl? Don't you know who I am?"

She clenched her jaw in a stubborn gesture and scowled. "Aye."

He lifted his chin at her. "Tell me. Tell me who I am."

"Lord Dain d'Ange, one of the Aviat thirteen rulers of the New Ecasian territory of Aeoli. You are descended from the son of Lord Rue and Lady Lilane, who was one of the first of the magicked ones. You are the lord of Aeodan Keep. When Ecasia went to war with the country of Laren'tar, you helped to lead our forces to victory. Your deeds are talked of throughout the land, carried forth by the bards. You were a hero during the war."

Dain shook his head. "No, girl. Tell me who I really am. Tell me the dark part of the story. Tell me about what happened when I came home from the war. Tell me what you've been told during dark, stormy nights by your friends and your family. Tell me the horror story. Go on."

She gripped the bars until her knuckles were white. "You are the thirteenth lord of Aeoli, some call you the cursed prince. They say you went mad from your experiences in the war and came back still afflicted by them." Her voice lowered. "They...they say you came back and killed your wife, Andreea, with dark, twisted magick. They say when it happened every bit of glass, every window, all the pottery...shattered...just like your wife."

"Then what in the name of Goddess Ariane are you doing here?"

"I-I'm not sure."

"Are you daft, then?"

Her lips twisted in a slight smile. "Though there are those in my village who may debate the point, I am not daft, my lord."

"The daft never know they are daft, girl. Others must judge. I judge that you must be insane to wish to spend your time here, alone, with me. Any length of time at all. Understand?"

"I am not daft and I do understand, my lord, but that doesn't change my needs."

Need.

The woman knew nothing of need. Not the way he did.

He stepped closer to the gate, raking his gaze up the length of her. He couldn't see much under the folds and billows of her winter clothing, but he had a good imagination. Her frame appeared slight, so it went to follow that her breasts would be small with suckable little red nipples. Her sweetly smooth and creamy flesh would probably flush when she was aroused. His fingers curled a little as he contemplated holding her breasts.

Her legs were long and probably lightly muscled, perfect for wrapping around a man's waist while he was buried balls-deep inside her pretty little pussy. He thought about how she'd taste on his tongue. How the muscles of her tight little sex would grip his finger, his tongue, his cock.

Dain shuddered in arousal, while his body responded to the images of her beneath him on his bed. How all her long red hair would spread over the pillow, how it would feel brushing over his thighs while she sucked his cock and how he could bury his hand in it at the nape of her neck and…

Abruptly, he turned. "Go," he commanded gruffly. "Stop this foolishness and get yourself far from me."

"My lord!"

He stepped away from the gate, headed back to his keep and his bottle of ale. "Blix, Athna, come." Blix looked back at him, whining, and Athna laid her great head on her paws. He turned and walked away. "Fine. Stay with the crazy woman, then," he called back.

"My lord, please! I must talk with you. It's of incredible importance!" she called.

Of importance to her, not to him. Though she sounded so desperate he almost felt bad for her when he turned the corner and walked out of hearing distance.

Almost.

* * * * *

Moira uncurled her fingers from the bars of the portcullis and dropped her hands to her sides. Well, it hadn't been as though she'd expected him to welcome her. She didn't know what she'd expected, but it hadn't been anything easy.

And it wasn't as though she could tell him that she'd been having blindingly painful psychic attacks in which his face and name were burned into her mind. It wasn't as though she could simply blurt out, "Who is Lord Cyric and what is your connection to him?" just like that. She felt intuitively that this situation required a subtler handling.

She stared past the portcullis, down the small road that likely led into the courtyard of Aeodan Keep. Tall, sun- and rain-kissed stone walls rose on each side of the entryway. The wind whistled down the pathway, but for that there was complete silence. For a moment she flashed to a time before. The smell of horse sweat and leather reached her nostrils and she heard the jangling of mail and horse's hooves on the gravel road. Beyond that came the sounds of a healthy and prosperous keep, merchants shouting to each other, children crying, conversation and laughter.

With a sharp shake of her head, she snapped herself out of it. Something horrid indeed had occurred here, and it did directly involve the keep's lord and master. But Moira had sensed no ill intent emanating from the man. She had no sense of dread when she said his name or saw his face.

No.

He was angry. He was dark. He was consumed completely by his past. But Moira knew instinctively that he was not a danger, no matter what the bards sung. He may snarl and bark, but he would not bite. Her gut told her that. Her fear of coming here had all been for naught.

She fished a bit of flatbread out of her saddlebag, broke it in two and fed it to the two dogs through the bars. Then she stood and took her horse's reins to lead her down the path away from the keep.

Aye, he could be pushed a little, and Moira had a strong will and much patience.

Chapter Two

ರಾ

Dain sat in his great hall with a flask of wine before him. He glanced around him as he took a long drink. The huge hearth was cold, the rushes covering the stone floor had long grown stale and spiders had taken over the corners of the large room. As the wine warmed him unwelcome memories from years ago danced through him. Gentle chaos used to rule here on warm summer evenings when the ale flowed, the men chased the women and the women let themselves be caught. Now when a person merely sighed it echoed through the room. Now the winter winds rattled the ice-kissed windows, and a layer of snow coated the ground. Now all the people were gone, and that was a good thing.

But still the woman remained.

She'd set up camp on the moors that lay just beyond Aeodan's battlements and had been there for a week now. He could see her campsite from the window in his bedchamber. Even in the dead of night, he could see her fire flickering beyond the glass, the stars bright above her head. It was as if she'd known exactly where to go that she might lodge herself in his awareness — or perhaps his conscience — the most effectively.

Every night he watched her campfire, while the man he used to be tugged at his mind. That man he'd lost so long ago urged him to bring her in from the cold. He whispered in Dain's head, telling him it was the right thing to do. He said that whatever fool's errand the woman was on she should not be allowed to sacrifice her life for it. Mostly, Dain ignored those thoughts. The woman should know that within

Aeodan's walls she'd be in far more danger. Better she should take her chances with the elements.

He took a last sip of his wine and pushed his breakfast plate away. Even now William prepared horses to go hunting. A long winter awaited them and they had not prepared enough for it. So far it threatened to be an especially harsh season. The snow had begun a week past and still fell nightly. They'd need extra stores of meat to salt and dry, extra wood for their fires. Extra everything. Especially since his brother Killian was set to arrive any day. Killian was his twin and about Dain's size, but Killian seemed able to put away twice as much food.

"They're ready, my lord," came William's voice from the entrance of the great hall.

Dain rose and joined him. He called for Blix and Athna who raised their great heads from their places on the floor near his table and together the three of them walked out of the keep and into the courtyard. Dain donned his riding gear, and mounted his horse. He and William rode past the barbican and out onto the moors that spread in front of Aeodan. His hounds loped gracefully through the snow beside the black gelding he rode, playing with each other and yelping for joy at being allowed on the excursion.

He and William rode far to the left of the woman's campsite. Still, he could feel her gaze heavy upon him as she huddled by her fire. Why didn't the wretched thing go home instead of freezing herself on the cold ground? He had nothing to offer her. She could have no reason important enough to cause her to risk her life this way. It was her decision, her choice and if he found her frozen corpse in the springtime he'd remind himself of that, the stubborn chit. He forced his gaze away from the direction of her campsite, toward the forest.

He gave his head a shake and examined the tree line rising before him, forcing his thoughts to the hunt to come. Hopefully they would find deer or elk today. The cold wind whipped at the exposed skin of his face. He blinked cold-singed, watery eyes. He could take to the air and scout for game, but one of the drawbacks of that was his size and wingspan. It tended to have the undesirable effect of frightening animals into hiding, though his eyesight was far more superior when he was in the air. He rubbed his chin, contemplating his options. When he looked back for Blix and Athna, it was to see them running the opposite direction.

Straight toward the woman's camp.

He reined up his mount and swore low and long under his breath. "I'll be back, William. Scout ahead for game and I'll retrieve my dogs." William nodded and Dain reined his horse around and with a squeeze of his knees, set it off at a gallop.

When he reached the camp, he saw the woman huddled in her massive swathes of clothing before her fire. She sat on a thread-worn blanket in front of a makeshift structure she'd constructed from branches. Over the fire was a kind of spit from which hung a small pot. Her horse searched through the snow nearby, pulling up winter-dry grass. Blix and Athna cowered next to the woman as he approached, as though they believed he'd harm them. It angered him. He'd never raised a hand to them, not ever.

"Blix, Athna," he commanded harshly. "Come." They didn't move. He looked up from Athna to spear the woman with his enraged gaze. His horse tossed his head and half-reared beneath him, sensing his rider's temper. "Are you magicked? Have you bewitched my animals?"

"I am magicked, but I did not enchant your dogs." She patted Blix on the head and flashed a smile. "They just like me."

There were very few of the magicked. They were the people descended from the First Children, those born right after the Goddess Ariane had broken her curse on the Sudhraian and Nordanese. The magick progressed down the lines of the First Children in a random way, manifesting like blue eye color or brown hair. Although the Aviat had never been touched by the Goddess' curse, they had also inherited the magick of the First Children.

Dain was also magicked. It was his greatest curse. It was a dark force within him that he kept carefully leashed. If he could reject the magick inside him, he'd do it in the blink of an eye.

Dain narrowed his eyes at the woman. He didn't trust magick, not a bit. "If you are indeed magicked, how am I to know you're telling me the truth? Perhaps you've bewitched Blix and Athna as a way to win me over and secure passage into my keep?"

She looked up at him. "But, my lord, you are also magicked, are you not? Why don't you simply look into my mind or emotions to see that I am not?" She resumed stroking her hand down Blix's sleek head and shoulders.

He suppressed an angry growl. "I don't ever use my magick...*not ever*," he finished with a snarl. "Not since—" He snapped his mouth closed.

She paused petting Blix and looked up at him for a long moment. "Do you feel me to be a threat? It is you who are the cursed thirteenth lord of Aeoli and is believed to have murdered your own wife. We have already established this, have we not? Therefore it is I who takes the risk, no?"

"What do you want of me?"

"Only an afternoon to talk with you." She eyed the bow and quiver strapped to his saddle. "If you are hunting, I may aid you. Perhaps we can talk while we ride."

He gave a rusty-sounding laugh. "You know nothing of hunting if you think we can talk during it. We would frighten the game." He eyed her slight frame. "In any case, how could you possibly help us? Can you shoot a bow?"

"No."

"Can you use a knife or haul heavy loads?"

"I cannot."

"Then how to do expect to aid?"

"With my particular magickal skills I can tell you where the beasts roam in the forest and help you locate them better than any tracking method you may have." She inclined her head. "I understand that as an Aviat you have superior eyesight, but my sensing ability will be even more an aid than your sighting skills."

He paused, pursing his lips together. He should say no. He should allow her no way into Aeodan, and yet... "If you can help us bring in meat for the winter, you will have a place at my table this eve and a chance to talk with me, if that is what you desire. A meal and no more. You will be forced to leave this evening afterward. No more camping on the moors. You will have to return home before the Aeolian winter truly sets in."

She stood and shook out her heavy gray skirts. "Agreed."

The three of them traveled through Aeodan's forests for the better part of the morning. William had hooked a small cart to his horse and deposited it by the tree line in order to more easily haul back firewood and meat. Well-trained, Blix and Athna were silent when they headed farther into the woods. All that could be heard were the crack of branches under the horses' hooves and the creaking of saddle leather. William and Dain both had bows ready, arrows notched and ready to fly.

The inclusion of the woman in the hunting party caused Dain to decide that he would not fly above the forest to spot prey. He'd inherited the wings of an owl as his Aviat birthright and the hunting instincts of one as well. Today he would allow the woman to use her magick. In spite of himself, she intrigued him.

Beside him rode the woman. She'd gone still as the surface of a pond on a breathless summer's day. Tuned in to the forest, perhaps. Finally she whispered. "There."

He glanced at her. She pointed almost straight ahead, a little to the left. He squinted, seeing nothing. Then the barest flicker of movement caught his eye. A bush moved. Dain squinted. It looked to be a boar rooting through the forest floor in search of food.

Too bad for the boar that they were also searching.

On his other side, William glanced at him, lowered his bow and took up the spear secured to his saddle. They communicated silently. Dain was the better shot with the bow, William would go in after with the spear.

Dain drew in a breath and raised his bow. Contrary to the tales of the bards, he did not relish the taking of life in any form, be it animal or human. Not even the owl within him could overshadow the human in this respect. He would take the boar because it meant their survival for the winter and for no other reason. The boar drew closer, oblivious to their presence, and Dain drew a line of sight and let fly. With a squeal, the boar went down. William rode in after to put the boar out of its misery. The beast went still.

The woman leapt off her mount, went to the boar and knelt. She placed her hand to the beast's side and looked up, her lips moving as she spoke something low. Dain watched her there on her knees in the snow, letting his gaze slide up the slender arch of her neck and the curve of her cheek. She had beautiful lips, he noted, full and soft.

She ceased her prayer and stood.

"What did you do?" he asked. His voice came sounding harsh to his own ears.

"I thanked the beast for the sacrifice of his life and gave my thanks to the Goddess and God for providing it."

Dain's horse moved beneath him, stomping his hooves on the ground. He regarded her silently. "What is your name?"

"Moira."

"You've earned a spot at my table this eve, Moira."

* * * * *

The minute Moira entered Dain's keep, a plump, red-faced woman ran up to her. "My dear lady," she exclaimed with a smile. "I'm so relieved Dain has invited you in." The older woman gave Dain a sharp glance full of reproof. "I feared he never would."

Moira looked from Dain to the woman, expecting him to snap at her, but he only calmly continued his work of divesting himself of his bow and quiver, which he set on a nearby table. "Moira, meet Bess," he said without looking at either of them.

"It's absolutely frigid out there! I watched you at your camp every morning and feared for you," Bess said as she fussed with Moira, pulling her heavy cloak from her shoulders.

It was still cold within the stone keep, but it was much warmer here than on the windy moors. A small fire sputtered fitfully in the hearth, not enough to warm the cavernous room. "I am strong, Bess," Moira replied with a smile. "I was passingly well on the moor, but thank you for your concern."

Beside her, Dain muttered something about stubbornness. Moira ignored him.

Bess glanced down her body and tsked. "Hardly. You're frail as a swallow. Anyone can tell that even with all the wrappings around you." Bess pulled at her arm. "Let the men see to the firewood and the rest. We will draw you a nice warm bath before dinner." She flicked another hard glance Dain's way and sniffed. "We'll demonstrate we can still show hospitality at Aeodan."

Moira looked at Dain, but he seemed to have forgotten all about her. She shrugged and allowed Bess to pull her away.

Bess led her out of the great hall, down a corridor and up a flight of stairs, prattling on all the way. "There are still some of us left, mind you. Myself, I cook for Lord Dain. My husband, William, does all sorts of odd jobs. Dain's brother, Killian, lives here most of the year, as well. Killian is away at the moment, but is due back any day now. We're sticking by his lordship, waiting for him come out of…well, whatever it is he's in." She heaved a sigh. "He was wrongly accused, I've always said. Wrongly accused."

Bess led her into a bedroom—one of many vacant ones, Moira supposed. A four-poster bed dominated the chamber, hung with heavy red taffeta curtains. A wardrobe stood adjacent to the hearth, where a fire burned merrily. A tub stood in the corner, half-filled with water.

Moira frowned, looking from the hearth and water-filled tub to Bess.

"I took the liberty when I saw you riding in over the moors with Lord Dain and William. I hope you don't mind."

"You pulled up all that water and heated it by yourself, Bess?"

Bess shook her head. "Don't trouble yourself. There's a well and bucket at the end of the hall. Really, it wasn't much a bother."

"You're so kind, Bess. Thank you."

Bess gave a little squeal of rapture that startled Moira. "I'm so happy to have another woman at Aeodan. It's been so long." Bess hurried out of the room and came back a minute later with a gown draped over her arms and a pair of slippers in her hand. "I don't know if they'll fit, but I thought you'd enjoy getting out of those clothes."

Moira took them and offered a smile in return. "More kindness. I can't tell you how thankful I am."

Bess patted her arm and winked. "Just having you here is thanks enough."

The servant woman aided her in undressing and then helped her into her bath. As Moira bathed, Bess bought several more buckets full of water, heated them over the fire in the hearth and added them to the tub. Moira scrubbed herself until her skin glowed, then got out and dried her body and hair with the towels Bess had provided.

The light pink gown was of soft wool and was a bit too large, though the slippers fit her perfectly. When Moira had just finished drying her hair by the heat of the fire, Bess called her to dinner.

The servant woman led her through a series of corridors, not to the great hall where she'd first entered the keep, but to a small room just off the kitchen. She supposed it was easier to keep warm. It was definitely less lonely-feeling and far fewer spider webs decorated the corners. One table stood in the center of the fire-warmed chamber. Fresh rushes covered the stone floor and tapestries hung the walls on either side of the hearth.

Dain stood when she entered the room. "Moira," he greeted her.

"My lord."

"Don't call me that. Just call me Dain."

"Dain, then," she replied and inclined her head.

He motioned to the chair across from him. "Please, sit."

She sank down into the chair and felt his gaze heavy upon her. It seemed to take her in from the tip of her toes to the crown of her head. It felt heated and seemed to almost caress her skin. Lust flared along her body, coming from Dain. She'd felt his desire before, when she'd talked with him through the portcullis. He was clearly attracted to her and her own body answered in kind. It was dangerous. She had to remember how long this man had been alone, sequestered by choice in the castle.

Abstinence was not a normal state of being for a Nordanese or an Aeolian. Both were highly sexual people, brought up in a highly sexual culture. She herself had been too long without a man and could feel the need of it within her body like tinder ready to catch fire. The last thing she needed was for it to ignite with this man across from her. He was very good-looking, but far too intense in temperament for a causal encounter. She looked up and held his gaze evenly. She was here on business, nothing more. It was better he understood that.

Bess served a simple dinner of boiled turnips and salted fish likely caught from the nearby Soren River. There were so many things she wanted to ask Dain, but she felt she should not. Why had he sent away all his men? What exactly had happened when he'd returned from the war? Why did he allow people to believe he was insane when he clearly was not? But these questions had naught to with the real reason she was here and would satisfy her own curiosity, only. As the wine disappeared down her throat and the food vanished from her plate, she knew she was running out of time.

"Tell me about your magick," he said.

She swallowed her sip of wine. "I developed the ability to read people about five years ago. My magick lay latent in my body and simply bloomed one day. I can see into the pasts of people and into their presents. Sometimes I even have a little precognitive insight into people's futures. The people of my village sometimes pay me to counsel them." She shrugged. "That's how my magick has manifested so far, at least. It is not very strong, in all honesty."

"What did you do before your magick manifested?"

"I lived in the village and worked in my family's horse training business."

"That explains your ease with a horse." He raised a brow. "And perhaps my dogs, too," he finished in a tight voice.

She felt a flicker of amusement from him despite his dour expression. She laughed. "I don't know why Blix and Athna have taken to me."

"You don't live in your village anymore?"

She shrugged and looked up. "No. Once the magick was in me, I found the constant presence of people to be grating. Back then I couldn't control my abilities very well and I could feel their emotions when I did not wish it."

"You're an empath," he stated flatly.

She felt a solid wall go up between them. No longer could she feel even a whisper of his feelings. "Yes. I'm descended from Lady Sienne." She was a recognizable figure in the history of New Ecasia since she'd played a role in how the Sudhrain–Nordanese war had begun and her mate, Marken, had played an instrumental role in ending it. "The magick within me started acting strangely about two weeks ago. I began having psychic attacks."

He leaned forward, but it was the only outward signal that he wanted her to continue. Moira caught a flicker of intense interest flare past the barrier he'd constructed between them.

"It started about two weeks ago," she continued. "I began seeing your face in my mind's eye and hearing your name at the same time. I call them attacks because they're very violent. They've become steadily worse. They're better since I've been here, so I know I'm on the right track."

He tapped his finger against the side of his goblet. "But you and I have no ties. Why should you be seeing my face in these attacks?"

She shook her head. "I don't know why. We've never met. I don't understand why we would be bonded in such a way. But there's more. I've been seeing another face and another name for far longer than yours." She hesitated.

"Go on."

"Do you know anyone named Lord Cyric?"

His face clouded and a muscle worked in his jaw. A wave of powerful rage rolled off him. It made Moira slide her chair back away from the table. "So he sent you, did he? Did he pay you a lot for this?"

Her eyes grew wide. "No. Please don't think that."

Dain stood. "You can leave now. I'll have Bess get your things."

"No, wait. Please listen to me." She stood. At the same time she rose pain shot through her head.

Oh, no. Not now.

A vision of Lord Cyric filled her mind and with it came the sensation of nausea. She dropped to her knees beside her chair and grabbed its arm in a desperate attempt to avoid passing out. Her hair fell across her face like two heavy blood-red curtains. She heard Dain raging above her, but his tone soon became concerned. She felt his hands on her upper arms at the same time the pain peaked and exploded through her.

Darkness followed swiftly, sucking her beneath the black with a power she could not fight.

* * * * *

Dain stared down at the crumpled figure on his floor and swore softly under his breath. Goddess, was this some kind of trick? Was she faking this? Had she been sent by Cyric to torment him? He knelt beside her. She was motionless, but still breathing. It appeared she'd passed out. He brushed several tendrils of her dark red hair away from her face. If she was an actress, she was a damn fine one.

Bess bustled through the doorway with a plate full of warm bread, screamed and dropped the platter. "My lord, what's happened?" She gave him a look of horror.

"I didn't do a thing to her, Bess," he said.

She scowled. "I was never thinking you did, my lord. Do you think I'd stay here if I believed you a menace?"

"She spoke of having psychic attacks. I think she may have had one just now. She's magicked."

"She's a descendant of the First Children?"

"That's what she told me."

Bess knelt beside Moira and felt her forehead. "She's in a deep sleep. We had better get her to a bed." She turned to Dain and snapped. "And I swear to the Goddess herself, Dain, you turn this one out into the cold and I'll take William and we'll leave you for good and forever." She shook her finger under his nose. "Don't you dare doubt my words!"

Dain picked Moira up. She weighed two ounces more than nothing. She needed to be fed. "Calm yourself, Bess. I won't turn her away." Unless Cyric has sent her, he added silently. Then she could freeze right beyond his front gate and he'd watch while she did it.

They brought her to the chamber where Bess had drawn her bath and put her into the bed. Bess and William built the fire while Dain contemplated the woman. Firelight flickered over her features as she lay there. Her long dark red hair was spread out over her pillow. He'd noticed her eyes right away. They were green and snapped with intelligence. Her body was slight, nearly weak-looking, though the woman had a tenaciousness that let him know that *weak* was not a part of her personality.

Beyond what she looked like on the outside, she had an evenness to her, a sort of *peace* about her. It seemed to emanate from her and wrap him within it, whether or not *peace* was what he wanted to feel. Peace was the last thing he deserved to feel.

He turned away and walked to the night-darkened window. The wind had picked up and snow now collected in the corners of the sill. He stared out as though to see through the darkness.

Thoughts of the past swarmed through his mind and made him clench his fists. "Where are you, Cyric?" he murmured.

Chapter Three

🔊

Moira opened her eyes just wide enough to see the red canopy draping the bed she lay in. She struggled to sit up and pain sliced through her head and shoulders. Wincing, she lay back into the pillows. She'd been so silly to assume the attacks had left merely because she'd come here. On top of it, that one had been the worst she'd ever had. She stared at the fire in the ornate hearth and sighed. What did The Powers want of her?

She had no ties to this place, to these people. Why was her life—such that it was—being so disrupted? She was descended from the First Children, yes, but by a roundabout way. She hadn't inherited any riches, or lands. She was a commoner, leading an unremarkable life.

That was, until now.

She closed her eyes. Goddess...she just wanted to go home. Home to her little cottage and her herbs.

Again she tried to push up, this time very slowly. She slipped her legs out from the blankets and her bare feet to the cold floor. It took her a few minutes to feel confident enough to stand. Finally, she walked with slow, measured steps to the window...and was met with blinding white. Snow blanketed everything beyond the glass.

"Feeling better?"

The low, smooth voice came from the corner opposite the bed. A shiver ran up her spine at the sound of it and she stiffened at the flood of *Dain* she suddenly sensed in the room. She hadn't felt his presence at all when she'd awoken, maybe because of her headache. Slowly, Moira turned.

Dain sat in a chair in the corner. The firelight illuminated half his face, leaving the other half in darkness. His dark eyes were intent on her. He had an all-consuming way of looking at her that left her mouth dry and her knees weak. It made her wonder what it would be like to be the sole focus of that intensity when they were both naked and in the bed to her left. Her stomach did a little flip-flop and she grasped the back of a chair near her for balance.

"Are you all right? Should I help you back into bed?" he asked in his silken voice.

She swallowed hard and tightened her grasp on the chair. "You startled me. I thought I was alone."

He inclined his head a degree. "I apologize. Are you feeling better?"

She steadied her gaze. "I didn't manufacture that episode last night as a ploy to remain here. Let's get that out of the way first."

"Moira, the idea had crossed my mind, I won't lie, but I believe you. I don't think you manufactured any of it. I watched you all night long and you didn't move, nor so much as whimper, until just now. If you faked that immobility, you must have the training of a monk of Anot. Now, how are you feeling?"

I watched you all night long. Her stomach did another little flip at those words. "My head still hurts and I'm a little unsteady on my feet, but otherwise fine." She pressed her lips together. "I can leave this morning if you like."

A silence descended. Moira waited for him to tell her to leave, to turn her out into the snow and cold without the information she'd come here for. She could feel nothing of his emotions. This man was accomplished at blocking them from magick-touched empaths such as herself.

"You're trapped here now, Moira. Trapped by the winter until the springtide," he said, finally.

Moira glanced out the window and clasped her arms over her chest. "I could still travel," she replied with a note of uncertainty in her voice. She didn't want to remain here if she wasn't welcome. She bit her lip. Anyway, she wouldn't say it out loud, but it was important she find Cyric. For all that, she knew he was right about her being trapped.

"Not with those attacks you're having. You might not be able to get through that cold and snow regardless of your condition. My brother Killian is a proven, blooded soldier accustomed to traveling in the Aeolian winter and *he* might have trouble getting through that early storm that hit us."

"I'm sorry to impose."

"Moira, I don't understand what's going on here, but I think I overreacted last night. You took me off-guard by saying his name. It's one I try not to think of very much and one that hasn't been spoken aloud at Aeodan in a long time."

"I don't understand what is going on either, Dain, and I don't know how I even *know* his name, or why." She gave her head a shake and regretted it when a pain lanced through it. "I don't understand the connections here."

"Maybe we can figure them out."

She closed her eyes for a moment. Thank the Goddess, he was going to help her. "I hope so, Dain. I really do. Believe when I say that all I want is to fulfill whatever it is The Powers want of me so I can go home to my cottage in peace."

He stared at her for several heartbeats in an assessing way, his eyes reflecting the firelight. "I will have Bess prepare a breakfast for us." He nodded and stood. "And I'll tell you of Cyric."

* * * * *

She wore a white woolen gown that was too large for her. The wide neckline slipped from time to time as she moved and dipped low enough to expose her collarbone and the smooth round of her shoulder. Bess must've have procured a store of clothing for her, Dain thought as he broke another bread roll in half and spread butter on it. Moira seemed unaware of the too-large size of her gown and his interest in the way the collar kept slipping down. It had been a long time since he'd seen a beautiful woman. It was only natural that he found her attractive.

Even when she'd been unconscious the night before and he'd spent long hours studying the rise and fall of her chest, the gentle curve of her cheek and the fullness of her lips, he'd fantasized about her. He'd been so long without a woman that she tempted him unmercifully. Last night in her firelit bedroom, he'd imagined slipping his hands under the blankets, under her clothing and running his fingers over her breasts, her sex.

He imagined teasing her body unmercifully until she creamed for him, came for him, until she woke and begged him to take her. How soft and tight her perfect little pussy would feel around his cock. How her moans would ring in his ears as he took her slow and easy at first, then faster and harder until the whole castle filled with the sounds of her cries.

His fist tightened on the stem of his drinking cup as an image of her spread, bound and at his mercy rose up in his mind. The thought fired every nerve in his groin. If only she knew everything he dreamed of doing to her, all the sexual games he wanted to play with her sweet body. Things that had been acceptable in the Nordanese noble class a century ago but were less practiced now and were especially erotic and foreign to a commoner. She'd run from Aeodan Keep right now, harsh Aeolian winter or not.

He took a deep drink and cleared the fog from his brain. It was only a self-torture to allow himself to think of such pleasure. She was off-limits to him. She was not his to seduce and she never would be. He would never be allowed such a treasure in his life again.

"Cyric," he started abruptly. She looked up from her breakfast of honey-drizzled bread and tea.

He didn't owe her the story he was about to tell. He didn't owe her anything, least of all the still too raw pain it would aggravate. Why did he wish to give her a blood-soaked piece of his personal history? He wasn't exactly sure. Only that the woman made him want to do and say things he wouldn't ordinarily.

"He used to be one of my landholders," he continued tightly. "He had a block of land to the south of here and a large manor house. He was a—" he couldn't help the sour expression that he knew had stole onto his face, or the fact he knew he'd choke out the next word "—*friend* at one time."

Moira had gone breathless. Her fork remained in her hand, stilled in mid-movement to her mouth.

He took another drink of his watered wine before continuing. "When I went away to war, I left Andreea alone. Since Cyric had a bad knee and couldn't go to war, he agreed to protect my lands and my wife in my stead." He felt a muscle in his jaw lock and took a moment to take in a deep breath before continuing. "When I came home, it was to find that he'd done much more than just protect her. He'd taken over *all* the duties of a husband."

"I'm sorry," she said softly.

There was more to the story, but he didn't want to reveal the darkest part. She knew it anyway. She'd already heard about how he'd come home from the war half-crazed by the bloodshed, the violence and the death. She'd also heard how, when he'd discovered his wife had been unfaithful, his latent magick had exploded outward from him in a killing frenzy, taking her life in a jealous rage.

"Where is Cyric now?" she asked.

"He fled. He left everything behind in an effort to escape my wrath. He took his stash of cash and jewels and ran. I don't know where he is."

She looked away. "Then I'm doomed."

A jolt of concern went through him. Goddess be damned! He didn't want to feel anything for this woman. He didn't want to feel *anything*, period. The last thing he deserved to have was emotion. Murdering bastards like him merited only numbness and misery.

He stood up. "If I ever found him, I would kill him," he said in a cold voice. "And I'm tired of killing."

She looked up at him. Her eyes shone with unshed tears.

Another stab of unwanted regard for her went through him. He looked away. "You can stay until the weather clears and the snow melts, not one minute longer. That won't be until the springtide. This is a big castle. Stay out of my way until then." He left the room in order to get away from the woman's big, beautiful green eyes, away from the feelings she seemed to be able to bring to the surface in him.

* * * * *

One day turned into two, two days turned into a week. Finally, an entire month had passed.

Moira sat at the end of one of the castle corridors. She drew her woolen blanket more firmly around her shoulders and stared out a large window that comprised part of the wall. She'd made it one of her frequently inhabited places. Here she could look onto the field that stretched in front of the barbican, her way toward home. The snow had hardly ceased to fall since the original storm that had trapped her here.

Snow and ice layered the ground to such a degree that she had no hope of traveling through it...if she ever had before. If she tried, it would be her death for certain not only because of the amount of snow, but also because of the intensely frigid temperatures that had descended over the land. The trees were coated in a layer of ice and when the sun went down behind them, it made the world appear as if it were made of sugar and crystal.

In the month since Dain had told her she could stay, he'd been true to his word and made himself scarce. She'd seen only glimpses of him as he turned a corner, or caught flashes of him through an upper-story window as he worked to train a horse in the snowy courtyard. Several times she'd glimpsed him from a window, swooping over the castle's turrets with his huge white owl's wings outspread. If it wasn't for Bess and William, Moira felt for certain she would've lost her sanity in the huge, lonely castle where every noise seemed to echo endlessly and the ghosts all seemed to crowd in on her late at night.

A blast of wind rattled the window and Moira hugged the blanket closer around her. At least she hadn't had any more attacks. Perhaps, at least for now, The Powers were satisfied with the steps she'd taken to see to their wishes, whatever they were.

Another blast of wind rattled the window, forcing Moira up from the chair. It grew too chilly to sit there staring out at the white world any longer. Deciding to continue her tour of the castle, which seemed never-ending, she sought the stairs and descended. She'd been up through the top floors of Aeodan, but she hadn't explored the lower floors yet. Her footfalls echoed on the stone steps as she went down and down, into the bowels of the keep. Would she find some chamber of torture down here? With a lord as strange and rage-filled as Dain, perhaps so.

Finally, the stairs came to an end. Here the corridors were dark because of the lack of windows. Her breath showed white in the air, though the temperature was slightly warmer here. The scent of mold and dampness made her nose twitch.

She paused, staring into the darkness. Why did she feel compelled to continue on? It was more than unpleasant here. Darkness and dampness weren't things she enjoyed, even if she was bored nearly out of her mind. Still, something pushed her to reach up and take a blazing torch from the wall and progress down the hallway, into the darkness. Maybe she'd go just a little way down the corridor. It wasn't as though she had anything else to do and...what in the Underworld was she thinking?

She halted and turned, shaking her head at her ridiculous inclination. The sound of footsteps on the stone floor made her stop and hug the wall. She knew the cadence of Dain's tread by now. Sweet Goddess, he didn't want to see her anywhere near him. He'd made that clear. She should leave. Moira moved toward the stairs with that intention. Then she heard him whistle a bit of an old Nordanese drinking song.

She frowned. Dain whistling? Maybe he was partially human after all.

Unable to resist her curiosity about what had put Dain in such an exceptionally fine mood, she placed the torch in a holder near her and inched her way past a series of wooden doors. Once past the circle of the torch's wan light, she reached out and dragged her fingers along the wall in front of her, feeling the grit and dampness of the stone. A light warmed the corridor farther up ahead and she moved toward it. Finally, she came to an open doorway. She crouched down and peered within the room.

Torches lit the walls of the large chamber, their light reflecting on a huge stone pool. A fount of water, perhaps from a hot spring, gurgled in the center of it. Dain stood near the edge, pulling his shirt over his head. Her eyes widened. His shoulders were broad and his chest was well muscled and tapered to a narrow waist. The muscles of his back worked as he removed the shirt and tossed it to the floor near him, next to his already discarded boots. His hands went to the buttons of his trews and she knew she should look away. Her hand tightened on the doorjamb. She seemed wholly unable to do that, however.

Dain dropped his trews to reveal a well-shaped backside and strong, muscled legs. Something low thrummed to life between her thighs. Her sex came to sizzling, pulsing life. Her heartbeat sped up and her breath caught in her throat. It had been a long time since she'd been with a man. She thought her libido had taken a permanent hiatus, but apparently it hadn't. She'd noticed Dain was attractive before. Any woman would, but now her body seemed to really take notice.

She watched as Dain stretched and turned. She caught sight of his cock, flaccid but still impressive. Sweet Goddess, the man was huge! Even at rest the organ was thick and long. In its erect form, it'd be positively frightening...or not. She could feel herself grow wet at the sight of him. A trickle of juice trailed from her pussy, down her inner thigh at the thought of taking that beautiful organ inside her.

Thankfully, Dain lowered himself into the water, concealing his body from her. Moira felt relieved and disappointed all at once.

"Moira, stop hiding and come in here."

She froze, shock and embarrassment ripping through her. Dain swam to the edge of the pool closest to her. Her gaze collided with his and her face heated.

"You should know it's impossible to stalk an Aviat," he said. "We have very acute senses. I've known you were there ever since you came down the stairs."

"Oh." She cleared her throat uncomfortably and stood. "I'm sorry. I was just exploring the castle and wandered down here. When I heard noises, I came to investigate," she babbled. "But I didn't want to say anything to you because I know you don't want to see me and—"

"Moira, it's all right."

She took a breath. "I'm sorry I spied."

He pushed off the side and backstroked to the other edge of the pool. Enticing glimpses of his body were visible beneath the foaming water, but she tried not to look...really, she did try.

"Why don't you make it up to me by coming in here?" he asked.

"Wh-what? In the pool?"

"Take off your gown and come for a swim. The water's very warm and it's filled with healing minerals. The water comes from a hot spring under the earth. It's good for a person in the middle of the cold season."

In the pool? Naked? With Dain? She might be aroused by this man's body, but his personality wasn't one she wanted to engage sexually. Her body wanted his, but her mind knew it was a bad idea to allow it to happen. "No, I couldn't."

"I can resist you. I'm not that uncontrolled."

For some reason that made her bristle. She put a hand on her hip. "I'm not taking my gown off in front of you."

45

He cocked his head to the side. "Your line is Nordanese, Moira. Are you really that divorced from your culture? Your antecedents practiced open loveplay in their lorddoms. Do you take shame in your nakedness just as a Sudhraian would?"

"It's not that." She took a step backward. "It's that I hardly know you and I far from trust you."

"So you fear me, then."

"Fear you? I don't—"

"You should fear me," he said a low voice. "I'm a murderer, after all." He turned away from her.

She took a step forward, shaking her head. "You're not a murderer." Those words were the truth. How she knew it, she couldn't say. She just did. No matter what this man believed, he hadn't murdered his wife. She felt that in her gut.

He stopped in the middle of the pool and regarded her silently. "I was there. My brother Killian was there. We saw her die with our own eyes. I held her in my arms as she did it and she cursed me with her last breath. There's no doubt I murdered her."

Moira shook her head. "My intuition is never wrong, Dain. I don't know what you saw, or what happened that day, but I feel strongly that you didn't kill your wife."

His eyes clouded with rage. "You're lying. You've been sent here by Cyric to torment me."

"No! I came here to find Cyric! I wasn't sent by him!"

"Then you're as daft as I first suspected." He turned away from her and began to swim away from her.

She made an enraged sound, pulled her gown over her head angrily and kicked off her shoes, leaving her clad in only her shift.

Dain swam back toward her. "What are you doing?" he asked.

"I'm coming into the pool," she said replied in a tight voice.

"I thought you didn't trust me."

She walked toward the edge of the water, still wearing her shift. It was a thin, white bit of clothing. Once wet it would be transparent, but it would be enough to make her feel like there was some kind of layer of protection between herself and Dain. She couldn't wear her gown in because if she got it wet, she'd catch her death walking back up to her chamber.

"I don't trust you," she snapped. "But how else can I prove that I really don't think you killed your wife?"

"Why do you think I care what you think?"

She huffed out an exasperated breath and stepped into the warm water and found the first of a series of smooth stone steps leading down into the pool. "You're completely insufferable, you know that?"

"So I've been told." He swam toward her and offered his hand. "Be careful."

She looked at his hand warily and declined it. "I'm just fine, thanks." She sank down into the water with a groan of appreciation. It really was wonderful. The heat seemed to sink down into every one of her muscles and release the tension she'd been holding in her shoulders and back.

The shift clung to her body as she swam through the water, and tangled around her legs. She wanted to take it off, but she didn't dare.

Dain stood looking at her from several feet away. His gray eyes had grown darker, they seemed...molten. What was he thinking? She swallowed the lump in her throat and returned his gaze steadily. "There, you see? Would I have entered this pool with you if I believed you a murderer?"

"If you were daft you would have."

She rolled her eyes. "You really are impossible."

"Why do you think I'm innocent? It is your precognition that tells you that?"

She shook her head. "No, it's more like a sense of knowing that I have about some things. It's my intuition. As soon as I met you at your front gates, I knew you'd never harm an innocent."

"I was in a war. I harmed and killed many...perhaps many of them were innocent."

She shook her head. "That's different. That's war."

"How?" he snapped, his eyes suddenly blazing. "How is that different?"

"I'm not here to engage in philosophy with you or debate semantics. When I came up to the gate I knew you were tormented, but not a murderer...at least you never murdered your wife."

He didn't say anything. He just looked away. "I would love to believe you, Moira. I truly would."

Her name on his lips made her body tighten and breasts feel heavy. Her mind played havoc with her for a moment, imagining him murmuring her name when he was thrusting deep inside her. She cleared her throat and backstroked away from him in order to get farther away. "This pool is wonderful," she said lightly, in an effort to change the subject. She turned and swam to the opposite end, then turned to do another length and came nose to nose with Dain.

He leaned forward, pinning her between his hard, lean body and the wall of the pool. His mouth came down on hers to hover a sigh away from her lips. Her heart thundered in her chest and her breath came harsh and heavy. "I guess you were right not to trust me," Dain murmured right before he bussed his lips across hers.

The light, bare brush of a kiss stole her breath. She searched for something to hang onto and found only Dain. Her fingers wrapped around his muscular shoulders and his hands found her waist, tangling in the wet material of the shift still encasing her body. He just hovered there over her mouth, just barely brushing her lips. Every single nerve in her body trembled at the slight touch, at his breath that bathed her lips.

A small, whimpering sound of need filled her ears and it took her a moment to realize that it came from her own throat.

Finally he ended the torment of it and with a little growl slanted his head and crushed his mouth to hers. At the same time, he pressed his chest to her breasts.

Moira's whole body came to screaming life. Her breasts became heavy and the nipples grew sensitive and erect as his chest scraped over them. The material of her shift was the only thing that separated skin from skin and the rasp of it over her sensitive nipples made shivers shoot up her spine. Dain worked his lips over her mouth, nipping gently at her lower lip, and then drawing it lazily between his teeth to pull on it. It tightened an invisible line straight to her pussy. She felt herself prime for him, her sex ready itself for his cock.

Dain coaxed her lips apart and slid his tongue inside her mouth. The first brush of his tongue against hers almost made her climax. He brushed up against her tongue slowly, methodically. The man kissed her like he looked at her, she thought with a shiver. Intense and all-consumed.

She shuddered and ground herself against his body in sudden need. Her hands drifted down, fingers exploring the ridges and valleys of his incredible chest and stomach. Her fingers closed around his hard, huge cock. She couldn't close her fingers all the way around his erection.

God, what would he feel like…

His hands coasted up, over her heavy breasts, teasing her sensitized nipples over the material of her shift. She groaned against his mouth as he slid one hand down. He found her clit and rubbed at it. Still the material of her shift separated his hand from her flesh. The material caused extra friction against her already overheated body.

Around and around he caressed, until she tipped her head back and could only pant and groan. His mouth came down on the exposed skin of her throat, nibbling and gently biting and kissing.

She cried out as her body tensed and climaxed easily for him. Pleasure ebbed out from the center of her, racking her body in wave after delicious wave. She'd forgotten how good it could be. It'd been so long since a man had put his hands on her. Finally the waves ceased, leaving her a mass of satisfaction and desire, leaving her wanting more of him.

His hands left her body and she opened her eyes, feeling half drunk and wanting only to draw him to her and drink her fill of him. She met his gaze and instantly stilled. Clouds of emotion swirled through his light blue eyes.

He jerked away from her. "Forgive me."

She shook her head, trying to form words, trying to tell him that it was all right. However, she suspected that offending her wasn't why he had that grieved look in his eyes. She felt regret roll off him and hit her in a cloying wave.

"I vowed to myself I would retain control. I truly thought I could. It's been a long time for me." He turned and exited the pool.

Moira grasped the edge of the pool, finally finding her voice. "It's been a long time for me, too, Dain," she said softly.

He stared at her for a long, stricken moment, and then left the room.

Chapter Four

ॐ

Dain sat in his chamber, his head cradled in his hands. A fire burned in the hearth across from him. It had been the first time he'd touched a woman since Andreea had died. He fisted his hands in his hair.

When Moira had pulled that gown over her head, all his fine ideas of control had vanished. Her skin was so soft-looking, so silky. Her feet were long and slender and led to delicate ankles and the beginnings of shapely calves that made him regret the shift she wore. He'd wanted to see the rest of those long legs so he could fantasize about how they'd feel wrapped around his waist while he was buried balls-deep inside her. He'd glimpsed her small, rosy nipples pressing against the thin fabric of her shift and when she moved just right, he'd been able to see the patch of red hair covering her sweet mound.

When she'd lowered herself into the water, the heat had made the distinct scent of her—hyacinth and some other flower he couldn't place—grow stronger.

That scent had haunted him over the last month. He'd smelled her near and would have to go in the opposite direction in order to prevent himself from doing something really irrational and stupid…like kissing her, or bringing her to climax.

Dain stood abruptly, walked to the fire and back. Killian would be so proud. He thought Dain had punished himself enough for what had happened when he'd come home from the war. That it had been an accident and thought he should take another wife and start over. Have children. Be happy.

Dain knew he'd never be able to punish himself enough. He'd never be able to allow himself happiness.

* * * * *

Moira rounded a corner on the lower level of the keep as she headed to the kitchens for breakfast. A week had passed since her encounter with Dain in the pool. She hadn't had even a glimpse of him since it occurred. If she didn't know better, she'd have thought he'd left Aeodan altogether.

Drawing her shawl around her shoulders against the chill, she entered the welcoming warmth of the kitchens. Moira stopped short as she saw Dain's dark head bent over a bowl as he sat at the long table that dominated the room. Blix and Athna lay on the floor near his feet.

Wasting no time, lest he disappear like one of the ethereal castle ghosts, she stepped forward, blurting out as she went, "Dain, please don't be sorry for what happened in the pool. I didn't invite it, it's true, but that doesn't mean I didn't—"

Dain lifted his head and she realized it wasn't Dain at all. He looked almost exactly like Dain, same dark hair, same light blue eyes, same handsome face, but there were subtle differences. The biggest difference was the contented light in this man's eyes, the marked lack of torment.

"Oh," she finished stupidly and closed her mouth. Blix and Athna whined, got up and went to her. She petted their sleek heads.

The man smiled and lifted a dark brow. "Something happened in the pool? I'm suddenly extremely jealous of my brother for the first time in many years."

She self-consciously brushed a tendril of hair away from her face. "I'm sorry. I had no idea you weren't Dain with your head bent down like that."

The man stood. "It's amazing you figured out I wasn't Dain at all. Usually no one can tell us apart." He walked toward her. "I'm Killian, younger brother by a minute and a half."

"Identical twins."

"Yes, but I got the better personality, I think." He winked and took her hand. He brought it to his mouth and laid a lingering kiss on it. "I didn't expect Dain to have such a beautiful visitor for the winter."

"I came right before the big storm and became stranded."

"Lucky for Dain."

A swell of sadness overtook her for a moment. "Unlucky for Dain. I think the last thing wanted was company. Most especially mine."

"Ah, but something happened in the pool, did it not? Apparently he's not so reluctant to share your company."

Her face grew warm and she didn't respond.

Killian muttered something uncomplimentary under his breath about his brother, then said, "Dain wouldn't know a propitious and happy occurrence if it bit him in the ass. He's too busy self-flagellating."

Bess bustled into the kitchen from the opposite end. "Ah, good, Killian, you're finally here!" She greeted Dain's brother with a matronly hug and kiss. "Thank the Goddess, poor Moira finally has some company other than myself and William."

Bess spent the next several minutes dishing up porridge for Moira and a second bowl for Killian. After she'd fussed for a while in Bess-like fashion, she finally went out of the room, mumbling about fresh bedding. Blix and Athna trotted at her heels, leaving her and Killian alone once more.

"So, you must tell me how you ended up in the castle of the crazed thirteenth lord of Aeoli, Moira. You're not daft, are you?"

She pushed the porridge around with her spoon. "People keep asking me that."

"Well, you must have heard the rumors about my brother. People don't seek him out very often."

"I've heard the rumors." She lifted her gaze to his. "Doesn't mean I believe them all. Doesn't even mean I believe your brother's version of the story. Doesn't mean I don't feel that he's innocent of the crime he self-flagellates himself for committing."

Killian paused and stared at her, a spoonful of porridge halfway to his mouth. "Well, now, that's intriguing. You must be magicked."

"I am." She lowered her gaze. "My full name is Moira ki Sienne."

"Descended from the Lady Sienne, herself? That's quite a heritage to boast."

"As is yours. Did you inherit the magick as well as Dain?"

He lowered his gaze to his bowl. "No. I have no magick as far as I know. Dain got both magick and Aeodan and does nothing with either."

"You sound bitter."

Killian looked up and gave her a half-smile. "I am not. Sorry for my brother, perhaps. I'm not jealous for what he has, just that he feels no desire to take pleasure in his good fortune."

Moira flushed and looked down at her bowl. That last comment seemed pointed directly at her.

"Tell me," she said after a period of silence. "Do you know anything of a man called Cyric?"

Every muscle in Killian's body went rigid. "Of course," he said harshly. "He cuckolded my brother when we were at war. He stole thing most precious to him in all the world, his wife. He accounts for Dain's downfall."

Moira pushed her spoon through the porridge in the bowl a last time, then set the spoon down. "The Lady Andreea had a part to play in it, I suspect," she said softly. Then louder, "I am searching for this man. Do you know where he is?"

Killian made a scoffing sound. "You search in vain. If anyone knew where he was, he'd be slain by my or Dain's hand by now."

Dain's voice came from the doorway of the kitchen, startling her. "Why do you persist so, woman? Let it go. He is better off far from Killian and I."

"Dain," said Killian, rising from his chair and going toward him.

Two men embraced, smiling and clapping each other on the back. "Was it difficult making your way here from Lord Arvand's court?" asked Dain.

"I almost didn't make it."

"Why did you leave? There are many pretty women to bed back there, no doubt," said Dain.

"Things are good there, but I am happy to be home for the cold season. I could use some peace and quiet. In addition, I find a pretty woman here." Killian motioned to Moira.

She stood, a hard expression on her face. "But I am not for bedding," she said primly. As she said it, she caught Dain's eye. All of what they'd done in the pool came rushing back at her, making her wet between the thighs, and she knew then that she'd just lied.

Killian just made the highly speculative sound of "Hmmmm". Was she that transparent?

She picked up her skirts and walked toward the doorway. Curse her pale coloring. She could tell her cheeks were flushed. "I have many things to see to," she said distractedly. She just needed to get out of there.

Killian gave a low laugh. "Yes, there's much to do in an empty castle in the middle of the frigid season, my lady," he called after her. "Things to do in the pool."

* * * * *

"How do you know about what happened in the pool?" murmured Dain, watching the beautiful Moira take her hasty retreat.

Killian smiled. "She thought I was you when she came into the kitchen. She said you didn't have to be sorry, brother." His smile widened. "Whatever it was you did to her, I think she liked it."

Dain's cock twitched in his trews. By the God Anot, so had he. He wanted more from her. He wanted her nude beneath him. He wanted her panting and moaning out her pleasure at his hands and mouth and cock.

"Why don't you take her, brother?" Killian asked softly.

He shook his head. "No. She didn't come here to be seduced. She came to me for insight, for help. It wouldn't be right—"

Killian held up a hand to stop his words. "My brother, always so worried about what's right. You're the noblest man I know."

Dain looked away to mask the flash of pain in his eyes. Noble? Not noble enough to stop the tidal wave of rage that had triggered his first and only manifestation of magick. The one that had shattered every window in the castle, destroyed everything made of glass or pottery and killed his own wife. "Do not talk to me of nobility," he ground out.

Killian sighed. "Well, if you're not going to take a shot at bedding the lovely, I will." Killian started to walk away. "It's a long winter, you know. Hope you don't mind. My Aviat nose does not deceive. The woman's begging for a long, hard tumble. Personally, I think she wants you, brother." He shot him a quick look. "But maybe she'll settle for someone who looks like you."

Dain lifted his head and stared at Killian's back as he left the kitchen. A curious jumble of emotions twisted in his stomach. He couldn't care. He shouldn't care.

But Goddess be damned, he did care!

Dain fisted his hands at his sides, but remained rooted in place as Killian's laugh met his ears and he started to whistle as he progressed down the corridor away from him. "Ah, it's good to be home," he called back.

* * * * *

The ghosts seem to follow Moira wherever she went in the castle. They whispered to her in voices just slightly too soft and low for her to understand. They caught up her clothing with barely tangible fingers when she turned corners. They breathed across her skin, making her feel as though she'd stepped through a cobweb when there had been no cobweb to step through.

Her talents didn't run to communication with disincarnates. Premonition, intuition, yes. Mediumship was a skill perhaps within her grasp, but yet still just out of reach. There was much about her power she hadn't explored, much she still didn't know.

The ghosts had secrets to impart. They had things to tell her and they seemed to desperately want to do that. However hard as Moira tried, she just wasn't able to hear them.

She turned a corner on the second floor of Aeodan and one of them smoothed across her cheek like a sigh. In some strange way, they comforted her. At least she wasn't alone. Moira sought the room she'd found a week earlier. It had been the ladies' solar at one time and fabric, spools of thread, weaving racks and yarn still remained. Several days ago, she'd set to cleaning up the dust and bringing the room back to rights. She'd been surprised that Bess had not reclaimed this chamber. Once the room was clean, she'd started on some new clothing. A pretty new shawl for Bess, tunics for Killian, Dain and William and a serviceable gown for herself. If she were going to remain here for the season, she might as well do something useful, something to earn her keep. Sewing and weaving had never been her activity of choice, but it was a far better alternative to slitting her wrists in boredom.

She settled down in a chair and picked up Bess' shawl. She'd begun embroidering a small, colorful pattern at the edges on it the day before.

As always, her thoughts turned to Dain. Every day she tried not to think of him, tried not to think of the tormented look in his light blue eyes. She tried not to imagine his lips on hers, his body nude, sliding against hers. She tried not to think about his hands on her body, driving and pushing her to a shattering climax.

It was hard not to think of him.

Sure as the ghosts in the castle, he haunted her. The scent of him, a woodsy-spicy scent, teased her nostrils when she entered an area of the castle where he'd just been. She woke in the middle of the night after having a dream in which he made love to her slowly, over and over again. It was a dream she had often. Her body would ache in neediness until morning, and bringing herself by her own hand was no good. It couldn't seem to satisfy the deep need she had for him.

Only he could do that.

Footsteps sounded outside the door. She scented him in the air and stabbed herself with her needle in surprise. "Ow!" she cried. She looked down, seeing blood welling on her index finger. She brought it to her mouth.

"Who gave you the right?" came Dain's voice, low and rasping.

Moira looked up sharply at the pained sound in his voice and frowned. Dain stood in the doorway, looking stricken…looking enraged. He glanced around the room and then leveled his gaze at her. Moira's heart nearly stopped at the look in his eyes. She wronged him somehow, but how…

"This was her room," he said in a low, cold voice. "You had no right disturb to it." He turned and walked away.

Stunned, Moira stared at the empty doorway for a moment, regained her senses, put the shawl to the side and ran after him. She followed him down the hallway at a quick pace as he stalked away from her.

"Dain, please wait," she called.

He stopped, but didn't turn around.

She reached him and put a hand on his upper arm. His shoulders hunched and his body tensed. She instantly removed it.

"You shouldn't have touched that room. That was her room," he said in a deceptively quiet voice.

"I-I'm so sorry, Dain. I didn't know."

"You should've guessed. I thought you were magicked. I thought you were intuitive."

"It doesn't make me infallible." She sighed. "I apologize, Dain. I know you want to keep her memory as intact as possible—"

He turned toward her and she swallowed hard at the hard look in his eyes. He took a step forward and she took a step back.

"Do you think that's why?" he asked with a strange smile playing on his lips. "Do you think that's why I don't want her things to be disturbed?"

"Uh, yes," she breathed.

He reached out and took a tendril of her hair between his fingers. He rubbed it back and forth, then brought it to his nose and inhaled. Dain closed his eyes and groaned. Desire spread out from her sex. Her breasts grew heavy and her nipples tight.

"Ah, god, you tempt me," he murmured. He slid a hand around her waist and dragged her flush up against him. She came willingly, fitting against his hard body like she belonged there.

"The thought of how you tasted and felt in the pool follows my every thought," he whispered near her ear. "I want to immerse myself in you, Moira. I want to bring you to my chambers and strip this gown from you. I want to lay you out on my bed and devour you, sink my cock inside of you."

Her breath caught in her throat at his words.

He brushed her hair away from her throat and laid a kiss to her collarbone. "In my dreams, I take you slow and easy and then fast and hard. I take you over and over from dusk until dawn, until we've both climaxed so many times we sleep for an entire day, naked and tangled together in my bed."

Moira closed her eyes. Her knees felt weak, but he was holding her up. His chest, smoothly muscled beneath his shirt, rubbed her aching nipples with every breath. His cock, huge and hard and straining, pressed through his trews and into her belly.

"You wonder why I don't want her room disturbed, my sweet Moira?" he murmured, his low voice rumbling through her. "It's not to preserve her memory."

Suddenly, he set her away from him. The harsh and abrupt action made her gasp.

He stood, silhouetted by the waning dusk light coming in through a window behind him. "It's so I remember that I might do it again."

He turned on his heel and walked away.

She watched him turn the corner at the end of the corridor, heard his footfalls fade away. "Oh, god," she whispered. Her knees finally weakened enough that she was forced to lower herself to the stone floor. Her body hummed and vibrated. Her pussy ached and felt so, so empty. How or why Dain had this power over her, she didn't know, but the man was going to make her go insane soon. "Oh, god," she breathed again, pressing a hand to her chest and feeling the fast pitter-patter of her heart.

* * * * *

Moira took a last look at herself in the long mirror in her bedroom before she left the chamber and descended into the lower floor of the keep. She'd closed the ladies' solar after her encounter with Dain, but she had taken her work to her room to finish. The next day she'd finished Bess' shawl and given it to her. The serving woman had loved it so much that she'd decided to call everyone in Aeodan together for dinner that evening.

Moira felt far from ready to face Dain tonight, yet she had no desire to offend Bess and therefore she had no choice.

She'd finished the gown that afternoon. It was a rich, deep green and made of soft velvet. It was a simple design with a square neckline and puffed sleeves. It fit her snugly until the waist, where it flared out into a gentle fall of a triple skirt. Something she could wear often.

Once upon a time, the Nordanese women had worn a material called flaxcloth. It kept the wearer warm, but was nearly transparent. In those times, the Nordanese had been under the curse of the Goddess Ariane and it had been especially difficult for women to conceive. In Nordan, this had fostered a culture that viewed sexual relations freely. Open sexplay was very common among the nobles and women and men copulated with many partners, very rarely taking monogamous mates. Sudhra, to the south, had been far more repressed.

After the war between Sudhra and Nordan had ended and the Goddess Ariane had lifted her curse, the cultures of both Nordan and Sudhra had changed. Nordan was still a bit freer in many ways than Sudhra, but the Nordanese no longer practiced open sexplay. Well, in most of the country, anyway. And the women no longer dressed in flaxcloth gowns.

She wore no jewelry and had secured her hair as best she could at the top of her head. Chiding herself for caring even a little about her appearance, she turned into the small chamber where Bess said she would be serving the meal.

All were already assembled when Moira arrived. All three men stood when she entered the room. Bess fussed and cooed and ushered her into a chair between Dain and Killian.

"Good evening, my lady," said Killian with a warm smile.

She nodded and smiled at him.

Dain said nothing and would not meet her eyes.

It was just as well, she didn't know what to say to him. She could feel him, though. Every breath he took and every slight movement he made seemed to go right through her. It was as though the very heat his body gave off warmed her through. They sipped their wine and talked of small things. William and Killian discussed what they'd plant in the small field to the left of the castle. She and Killian discussed the goings-on in the Port of Paradise and a bit of politics.

Suddenly, Dain stood, nearly knocking over his wineglass. "I am not hungry and will retire a little early this evening."

Stunned, everyone looked up at him.

Just then Bess bustled in from the kitchen with their first course. "You most certainly will not, my Lord Dain. You will sit down and act like the civilized lord of this castle for once." She clucked her tongue. "Your brother is here and you have a guest. The least you can do is take wine and break bread with them once in the same room."

Dain stood a moment in silence. A muscle worked in his jaw. Finally, he sank back down into his chair with a stone-like expression on his face.

A smile played with Moira's lips. She pretended to cough and covered her mouth with her napkin. Bess was a formidable woman. Perhaps she was the only person in the world formidable enough to control Dain.

Bess smiled. "Much better. Isn't this nice?"

Dain grimaced, but Moira thought he was actually trying to smile. "Very nice," he ground out.

Bess served a thin chicken broth with bread, then a roasted pheasant Killian had brought in with him.

By the final course, Moira was full of wine and laughter. Feeling more relaxed, she allowed herself to smile and joke with Killian, William and Bess. Bess served a beautiful sugar cake with white frosting for dessert. Moira took just a sliver since she was full from the delicious meal.

Killian cut a slightly larger piece of cake and added to her sliver. "Life is short, Moira. Come now, you must take advantage of pleasure when you have it served to you."

She laughed and picked her fork up. "You sound like my father," said Moira.

"Ah, yes, my lady," said Dain in a low voice. "But neither of us are your father. You'd best remember that." He got up and left the room.

* * * * *

"What is it about my brother that attracts you so?"

Moira turned from her place by a window, where she'd been watching the falling snow. She'd been deep in thought about many things. Her attacks had not gone away. She'd had two in the last three weeks. Every day she found seclusion, sought answers from The Powers. Every day she failed to find them. She'd been so deep in thought that she hadn't even heard Killian come up behind her. It had just been her, the ghosts, and her thoughts.

She gave him a distracted half-smile. "Why do you say I'm attracted to him?"

He laughed. "Because you get this funny look on your face whenever you're in the same room with him and you're avoiding him as much as possible."

"Well, maybe I'm avoiding him and have a funny look on my face when he's around because I don't like him. Haven't you considered that?"

"No," he said evenly. "I know you're attracted to him. I can tell."

She glanced away. "Is it that obvious?"

"You're attracted to him, but not to me. Why is that?" He spread his big hands and smiled. "We both look the same, after all."

"Attraction goes much deeper than looks, Killian." She tipped her head to the side and smiled. "Anyway, who told you I wasn't attracted to you? I am. Very much so, in fact." The truth was, she was physically attracted to Killian, but there was something more where Dain was concerned.

"Well, I'm glad to hear the last part, but you have to explain the first part. Ever since Andreea died, he's been more like a bear than a man." He shrugged. "What's to be attracted to?"

She didn't answer for a long moment. Instead she looked out the window. "Dain is a complicated man who holds the shadows close to him. By choice, he has cloaked himself in them. He's a good man who thinks himself evil. But, sometimes, in the depths of his eyes and the way he looks at you or Bess, I glimpse the man he should be, the one he was before Andreea died. It's that man I'm attracted to, but it's the whole man that enthralls me."

"You have eyes that see past the outer," replied Killian solemnly.

She looked back at him. "Come, you are his brother, not only that, his twin. Don't tell me you don't see what I see."

"When I look at Dain, I don't see his true self cutting through the darkness as you do." He shook his head. "When I look at my brother, I see a broken, tortured man and know that if I cannot somehow pull him back from the shadowed part of himself, I'll lose him forever. Time, Moira, time is running out for Dain. Don't you feel that?"

She glanced down and then back up at him. "I do." She held his gaze steadily.

In that moment, they forged a bond with the link of Dain between them. They both saw Dain in different ways, yet the core of their feelings about him was the same. They both cared for the same man and that gave them common ground and a connection.

"My brother told me of your problem, why you seek Cyric and why you sought Dain," said Killian.

"Yes." She folded her hand into her sleeves, as though trying to protect herself. "I've had the sight for a few years now, but these attacks are something new and they are not welcome at all."

"Is there much pain?"

She licked her lips. "Sometimes, yes. Sometimes I just pass out. Sometimes there is both agonizing pain and unconsciousness."

"It must be frightening."

"I would just like to know why I'm having them. There's a reason. There's something driving me toward Cyric and Dain." She shrugged. "The most likely explanation would have something to do with what happened on the day Dain came back from the war. What can you tell me about it?"

He smiled. "Well, that is a long story, but one I think you're entitled to, given your seeming connection to them both. It's a good thing I'm here. There's probably no way you'd ever get Dain to talk of that day."

Moira glanced out the window. She knew that was true. Her thoughts strayed back to the incident in the hallway a week ago and she shuddered. Dain had excited her body and crushed her emotions all in the same instant.

"Why don't you come with me? We'll go somewhere it isn't as cold, have something warm to drink and talk."

She nodded and smiled. "All right."

A little later, they found themselves seated in a small room off the kitchen. William had lit a fire for them and Moira had cuddled herself into a thick, warm blanket in a chair by the side of the hearth and held a mug of spiced cider in her hands. She closed her eyes briefly, enjoying the comfort. The fire, cider and blanket were finally driving away the chill that had seemed to permanently settle itself within her bones.

"My brother is not the best of hosts, as you've noticed," Killian said in a low voice. He sat opposite her. The firelight licked at his face and the dark shirt and pants he wore. If it weren't for the look of contentment in his eyes, or the slight difference in the lengths of their hair and the way they held their bodies, she wouldn't be able to tell them apart.

As it was, she could tell the difference between them at a glance, at a simple inhalation. Dain used a different soap when he bathed and the mere scent of it fired her blood.

"No, I realize that. However, it's not as if I were invited," she replied.

"He was ready to turn you out to the winter." His tone was light, but she noticed that he'd clenched his fist on his thigh. "He almost did turn you out." His smile grew tight.

"He let me stay at the moment I truly needed to," she answered lightly.

"You are far too forgiving, my lady."

"Call me Moira, please."

"If you will call me Killian."

She smiled. "Of course. Tell me, Killian, about your family first, will you?"

"Our family? There isn't much to tell. We're descended from Rue and Lilane. They're the ones who built Aeodan and established the Aeolian territory. They, along with others including Lord Talyn and Lady Raven, thought it was important the Aviats reclaim their heritage and culture. Aeodan had been passed on through the ages in our family."

"What were your parents like?"

"Were?" He smiled. "They're still alive. They live in the southern part of Nordan. They're very much in love, even after all these years." The smile faded. "Though Dain will have nothing to do with either of them."

For some reason she wasn't surprised to hear that. She took a careful sip of her drink. "Tell me of that day when everything changed. I understand you were there." She licked her lips. "That you...saw it."

Killian stared into the fire. "We'd returned from Laren'tar, from the final battle of the revolution. The lords of the three territories had finally formed an iron-strong alliance." Moira watched his eyes glaze over with the memories. His voice lowered when he continued speaking. "It was the worst battle of the entire war, the bloodiest. Dain was almost killed by a soldier loyal to the dictator. We fought back-to-back for the entire battle and when it was over, we walked through the burned-out, corpse-strewn battlefield together." He turned and looked at her with sorrow in his eyes. "We were happy to come home."

"What did you find when you got home?"

Killian sighed and set the mug to the side. He pursed his sensual lips for a moment, the same full lips that Dain possessed. "As soon as we cleared the gates, the servants besieged us, telling us of the affair between Andreea and Cyric. Dain was enraged by the betrayal and stormed into the keep. Andreea and Cyric were both there, in the bedroom together. Dain had wanted to surprise Andreea, so he hadn't sent a messenger ahead. No one had warned Andreea and Cyric, though the commotion in the courtyard had alerted them. They were dressing when Dain found them."

"And his magick manifested for the first time in his rage," finished Moira. She'd heard the stories.

Killian's face went pale. "It was an incredible display. The force of it broke every window, every bit of glass and pottery in Aeodan. It brought us all to our knees under the force of it. When it was over there was one dead and that was Andreea."

"And Dain blamed himself for it," said Moira.

"Everyone blamed Dain for it. They said he'd gone insane from the war, that he'd grown too comfortable with the taking of lives. Some of them left. Most he—"

"Drove away," she finished.

"Yes."

She took a sip of her cider and looked into the flames of the fire. "He's still trying to drive them away." She glanced back at him. "And Cyric?"

"He fled. He never returned to his holdings. I suppose he thought Dain would want to kill him for what he'd done. Dain might want to kill him, he might say he'd kill him, but he wouldn't." He paused. "I would, though. For being the cause of my brother's current state, I'd kill him."

She shook her head. "I still don't believe Dain killed Andreea."

"I was there. I saw it happen, Moira. My brother didn't mean to kill her, but he did. It was an accident born from rage."

She set her mug onto a table near her chair. "No. She died from something else, perhaps a sickness of the heart." She got up and went to stand by the door. She wrapped her arms over her chest against the chill emanating from the large, empty kitchen. "Perhaps Andreea died of natural causes," she finished softly.

"You are good to think it of him." Killian stood and walked over to her. She felt his huge hands cup her shoulders. The warmth of his touch bled through the material of her gown. She closed her eyes for a moment, wondering if Dain's hands would feel the same way.

Killian pressed his chest to her back and his voice rumbled through her when he spoke. "If you close your eyes, can you imagine I am my brother, Moira?"

Her breath caught in her throat. His voice was like a fine wine served in a velvet cup. For a moment, she wanted him with all her body and soul. Dain or not. It was like he'd read her mind, but then it was likely obvious what she desired.

His hands moved down her arms and he dropped his head, so he spoke near her ear. "Would you...want to close your eyes and imagine that I am?"

"I—" She didn't know what she wanted, but Killian's hands on her, his voice in her ear...ah, Goddess, it was good. It was good to feel the touch of another, a man's hands on her body. It would be so easy to give into the fantasy of it.

"If you close your eyes, you cannot see mine and you will not know that I am not Dain," Killian said. At the same time, he drew his hands down, brushing his fingertips over her nipples. They came to life, pebbling hard under the contact, becoming sensitive. She started but she didn't move away.

She was no maid and Killian had to know that. Loveplay, while not openly practiced as it was so long ago, still was something given freely by non-committed adults. Moira had been with quite a few men, though they'd just been dalliances, nothing more.

Never had she felt the way she did when Dain laid his hands on her.

She could imagine it was Dain who laid his hands on her now, that it was he who lay his lips to her throat for a gentle kiss, that it was his hands that smoothed down her sides and gathered her gown in his hands to lift it.

Her heart beat faster as she began to lose herself in the fantasy. Her breath caught in her throat. This could be as close as she could get to having Dain, but she couldn't do it.

If she was going to let Killian touch her and she was going to pleasure him in return, she had to do it without that particular illusion.

She felt the cool slide of her skirts smoothing up her thighs. Her mind said she should stop him, but she couldn't seem to verbalize it. Instead, she lifted her arms up and let him draw her gown over her head.

She stood in just her chemise, a thin white bit of fabric. Goose bumps made her shiver, but it was less from the cold air coming from the kitchen than it was from Killian's large palms slowly running down her arms to gently cup her breasts.

She swallowed hard and dropped her arms, bringing them back to touch as much of Killian as she could in this position. He shushed her and pressed her arms to her sides, then returned to pluck at her nipples. Killian kissed the nape of her neck and softly bit.

Her sex plumped as his teeth rasped against her sensitive skin. Her clit came to life. As if Killian knew what she wanted, he dropped a hand to bunch her chemise up and tease his bare fingers over her needy pussy.

Killian hissed out a breath. "You're already wet, Moira. So ready. You've spent the last weeks in agony, haven't you? Do you want me to touch you now? Give you ease?"

"Killian, yes," she hissed, using his name on purpose, reminding herself that this was not Dain, but his brother.

She closed her eyes as he urged her thighs apart and stroked his fingers over her clit, petting her until her breath caught in her throat and her pussy creamed for him.

Needing to give pleasure as well as receive it, she tried to turn in his arms. He stopped her with a grip of steel. "I want you in this position," he growled into her ear. He pointed at a nearby chair. "Put one of your feet on that chair and open yourself to me."

Moira lifted a slippered foot and rested it on the seat of the chair. Cool air rushed under her bunched-up chemise, bathing her hot, aching sex. In this position she felt completely vulnerable to him and that fueled her desire.

"So pretty," Killian murmured into her ear as he rubbed her swollen labia. He slid a finger inside her, then two, and she arched back against him. "Mmmm, it's good, isn't it?" he purred near her ear.

"Yes," she hissed.

"You're dying for Dain to do this to you, aren't you?" He slipped a hand under her chemise and stroked over her breast as he thrust in and out of her slowly. Killian rolled her nipple between his thumb and forefinger making it hard for her to answer. She felt ready to come at any moment. Having Killian's hands on her was so much better than bringing herself.

"Y-yes," she breathed.

He picked up the pace of his thrusts and ground his palm against her clit. "You're dying to have him spread your thighs and fuck you until you can't breathe, isn't that true? Can you imagine him doing that now, sweet Moira? Can you feel him thrusting inside you now? His breath hot on your neck, your heated body sliding against his?"

Moira shattered against Killian. Her climax hit her hard and spread out, enveloping her body in ecstasy. She felt the muscles of her pussy clamp down and release around Killian's fingers.

"Ah, that's what I wanted," Killian purred. He petted her sopping pussy as the waves of her climax ebbed and then stopped.

Moira turned, letting her chemise fall back into place and went down on her knees in front of him, determined to repay the pleasure he'd just given her. Just as she had her hands on his trews, he reached down and pulled her to her feet.

"No, Moira."

She regarded him for a moment, confused.

He closed his eyes for moment. "No," he said evenly. "As much as I want it, no. Go back to your room."

"But—"

"*Go.*"

After a moment of hesitation, she did as he wished. Perplexed by his behavior, she left.

* * * * *

From the shadows in the kitchen, Dain watched Moira run from his brother wearing only her chemise. He'd seen the whole thing and his cock was harder than he'd ever imagined it could be.

Goddess damn Killian! There was no way his brother hadn't known he was here watching. He'd done that just to tempt him, push him toward Moira. His brother was meddling...*hard*.

Dain watched Killian stand for a moment, staring after Moira. Then he also left.

Dain walked out from the shadows and stood near her dress. He swore long and colorfully under his breath and scooped her gown up. He lifted it to his nostrils and inhaled, closing his eyes. The scent of her could make a man drunk.

A mix of emotions swirled inside Dain as remembered what Killian had said to her about pretending to be him. How she'd come apart in his arms after imagining it was he who took her. Her cries had sounded so sweet. Her body had looked so ripe and tender. It had been all he could do to not go out and join his brother. It would not have been the first time they'd shared a woman.

Dain fisted his hand in Moira's gown. He didn't want to endanger her. Any women...*anyone*...who connected themselves to him were in danger. His magick and his emotions were passionate, volatile things. What if what happened with Andreea happened again? For their own protection, it was better if people just stayed away.

But the scent of Moira. The thought of her. The fantasy of her. These things haunted his every waking moment and his dreams. The curve of her cheek he imagined cupping in his hand. The swell of her breasts he imagined brushing his chest as she impaled her sweet sex on his rigid cock. It was worse for the power of his Aviat senses, for he could scent her arousal from a distance.

Through every dinner they shared, her scent drove him insane with need, kept his cock hard the entire time. Every time he glimpsed her in a hallway, chatting with Bess, William and Moira, the mere nearness of her made him crazy from desire.

It was impossible to have the woman in his castle and not want her. It was an unimaginable torture to deny himself the touch of her, especially when he knew she wanted him every bit as much as he wanted her.

What if it was just for one night? One night to rid himself of this lust he had for her. One night to drown themselves in the taste and touch of each other. Would it help? Would it help him get her out of his system? Then perhaps he could distance himself from her, to keep her safe from his volatility.

Dain closed his eyes, trying to resist the temptation…and failing.

Chapter Five

❧

Dain pressed her wrists to the mattress on either side of her head and hovered over her. His eyes were dark and his expression intent. Holding her gaze, he nudged her thighs apart with his knee and pressed the head of his cock against the slick opening of her pussy. It felt like a question. Her sex, already creaming for him, clenched in response.

"Do you want me, Moira?" Dain asked in his velvet voice.

"Yes, I want you," she panted.

"Are you willing to let me have you in every way...any way I choose? Do you still want me knowing I might take you in ways you've never been taken? Do you still want me knowing I might want to share you with another, watch as another man eases himself inside you?"

Her stomach fluttered. She paused for a moment, feeling the hard thrust of him against her, imagining that length within her, stroking into the softness of her. Oh, Goddess, she'd give anything. Anything he wanted to do to her she was ready to accept.

"Yes," she answered softly.

"You're willing to give yourself over to me completely, even knowing I might pose a danger to you?"

"Yes," she said evenly. She shifted her hips, causing him to rub his cock against her clit. They both groaned in unison. "Yes," she sighed. "Please, Dain, please."

Moira awoke with a gasp in the middle of the night. The full moon beyond her window reflected on the world of snow and lit the room in a silvery hue that warred with the light from the fire in the hearth.

Her breath came fast and hard and the remnants of the dream teased her already alert body. She snaked a hand down under the covers to touch herself and found bare need. She contemplated bringing herself to climax, but it would only leave her emptier and needier than before.

There was only one cure for this particular affliction.

She sat up, wondering what had awoken her, and pushed the bed warmers to the side with her bare feet. It was so cold outside that the fire and the bed warmers did little to bite into the frigidness of the room.

She glanced around the chamber feeling something foreign, a presence. Perhaps it was a ghost begging an impossible audience. Just then her gaze alighted on a figure in a chair in the corner. Her heart thumped hard in her chest. This need for him was growing tedious and his tempting her was growing unbearable.

The shadows half concealed Dain's face and the firelight flickered over him, licking at the exposed skin of his chest the way she wanted to.

"How long have you been there?" she asked in a shaky voice.

"You cried out in your sleep," he answered, without really answering. "You whimpered and you moaned and tossed your head."

She gripped the blankets to her chest. "I dreamt of you...of us."

His eyes flared with interest so brightly that it seemed she could see it even from across the dimly lit room. His hands were steepled and he sat slumped in the chair a little, as though he'd been there a while, made himself comfortable.

"How long have you been there?" she asked.

Dain didn't answer. He just sat there, staring at her with a gaze that seemed to leave her vulnerable and nude to the world.

"Leave, Dain," she said brokenly. "If you only mean to sit and stare and not to touch me, leave this room now. I cannot stand this any longer. Leave and torment me no more."

He sat for a moment longer, staring, and then rose. Her heart skipped a beat as her mind tripped over itself. *Please, don't leave. Pick up the challenge I've given you.*

"And what if I want to touch you, Moira?" he asked in a voice like a caress over her skin. "What then? Would you still wish me to go?"

She stilled as he took a step toward the bed. Unable to answer him, she could only watch as he moved closer and closer to her.

"Moira," he murmured. "Why do you want me? How could you want a man like me?" He stopped at the edge of her bed and stared down at her.

Anger suddenly overwhelmed her. She threw the blankets aside and slid out of the bed on the opposite side of him. The wood floor of the room felt icy on her bare feet. "Don't play with me this way, Dain," she said. "I care for you. I have from the moment I stepped up to that gate and you turned me away, silly woman that I am."

He spread his hands. "But why? Why me? Why a broken man, a murderer, like me?"

She stood staring at him. "I don't know." Moira stomped to the door and threw it open. "Just get out. I can't take this anymore. You make me want to flee into the Aeolian winter to escape you. You're far colder than the journey would be."

He walked to the door slowly. His every footstep sounded in the suddenly quiet room. She backed away as he reached the door, but he grabbed her around the waist and dragged her up against him. "I'm not always cold," he murmured as his mouth came down on hers.

Moira stiffened, then relaxed against him, fitting herself into the curve of his body. His mouth felt hard and hot on hers and the shock of it stole her ability to breathe for a moment. She made a low sound in her throat and rose up on her tiptoes, trying to embrace as much of him as possible, and returned his kiss ferociously.

Dain slid his hands around her waist and smoothed one up her back to tangle in the hair at the nape of her neck. His lips danced over her mouth, alternately parting her lips so he could allow his tongue to brush against hers. He tasted of mint and the woodsy, spicy scent of him made her half drunk. Her body, already teased further than any man had ever teased it, flared to life. He wouldn't walk away from her this time. All she wanted in the world was this man between the sheets of her bed.

The kiss was like no other she'd ever received. It was no kiss of mere desire. This was a possession. A taking of her breath and lips and tongue by Dain. She was more than happy to give it all up to him. She felt like she'd been waiting forever to do it. What's more, it felt utterly right.

He grabbed the edge of her chemise and drew it over her head. It fluttered like a sigh to the floor beside them. She stood completely nude while he was still dressed. There was something erotic in that. Something in it that made her feel vulnerable to him and it excited her.

He stood back and took her in from head to foot. The light in his eyes was far from cold when he again captured her gaze. The chill of the room didn't touch her. Instead, her flesh felt heated, eager. She moved to unbutton his shirt, but he grabbed her wrist and led her to the bed. He turned her toward him, pressing the backs of her knees to the edge of the mattress, and gave her a gentle push. She went down her back and he stood over her, looking down at her and taking in every square inch of her excited body.

He found her gaze and held it. Their eyes never left each other's as he undressed. He took off his shirt, slipped his boots off and dropped his trews. Finally, he crawled onto the bed over her, pinning her beneath him with his hands on either side of her head.

She broke his gaze then and glanced down at his chest. Long, thick scars raked the muscular bulges of his arms and his chest. From the war, most likely. With a finger, she traced the length of one, and then another. When she ran into a flat, male nipple she toyed with it until Dain shuddered.

"The war," he murmured. "The war marked me that way all over my body."

She pushed at his chest, compelling him to topple to the side. She rose up on one arm and smoothed the flat of her hand down his incredible chest. "You're beautiful," she whispered. She let her hand trail farther, until it tangled in the coarse hair around his shaft. She closed her fingers around the base. He was huge, much larger than any man she'd touched before, and hard as a rock. She wondered how many women he'd had since his wife had died. "So very beautiful," she said again as she stroked him with curious, questing fingertips.

Dain groaned and the sound reverberated through her. She leaned down and kissed his lips, his throat, then licked down a long scar, tasting the warm salt of his skin.

Abruptly, she found herself flat on her back. "My turn," he growled. He lowered his mouth to her breast.

She arched her back as his sensual lips closed around one of her nipples and his tongue laved over it. Dain groaned and closed his eyes. He slid his hand down her waist, over her hips to caress her outside of her thigh.

Moira trembled under his hands, her entire body unbelieving that it was finally getting what it yearned for all winter. Her aroused clit was plumped and so sensitive that the slightest brush would bring her to a shuddering climax. If his touch on her thigh alone could do that, she wasn't sure she could bear it when he caressed a more sensitive area. Her fingers closed around his shoulders and gripped as she twisted beneath him. His teeth rasped gently over her nipple and Moira moaned. "Please," she cried. "More."

Dain broke from her nipple and kissed her stomach, working downward. "What do you want, beautiful?" he asked. "What more do you want from me?"

She lifted up and looked at him. "I want it all."

He parted her thighs and settled down between them. Dain brushed his finger over her swollen sex as he examined her up close. He closed his eyes and groaned. "All? You have no idea all the things I want to do to you. Goddess, you're the most beautiful thing I've ever seen, Moira." He groaned. "Catch your knees in your hands and show me everything," he ordered. "Spread yourself for my gaze and tongue."

She hesitated.

"You said you wanted my all, Moira," he said darkly. "I'm very dominant in bed. If you want my all, you must be comfortable with that. You must do what I ask of you in the bedroom, whatever that may be. Do you agree?"

The dream she had came back to her. In her dream, he'd made her agree to submit to his whims, no matter how deviant. Something fluttered in her stomach, something that excited a dark part of herself. She nodded and did as he told her to do, stretching her knees back and up, giving him a completely unobstructed view of her pussy.

Dain groaned deep in the back of his throat. "I bet you taste so sweet."

"Lower your mouth and find out," she breathed.

"All in good time. The night stretches before us."

He ran his fingers over her folds and slipped a finger within her. With his thumb, he massaged her clit in a circular motion. A climax flirted hard with her body and she gasped and arched her back. He let up on the pressure on her clit. "Not yet. It must build to be truly memorable."

Goddess, he planned to torture her before this was through.

He inserted a second finger to join the first, stretching the muscles of her sex. Her eyes rolled back in her head as he pulled his thick fingers out and thrust them back incredibly slowly. Again he stroked her clit, making her body shudder.

She moaned and dropped her head back to the mattress, arching her back and stabbing her tight nipples into the air. Her cream fairly ran down her inner thighs.

"Do you want to come?" Dain asked in a low voice. "Do you want to drench my hand right now, Moira?"

"Yes," she answered gutturally. "Sweet Goddess, yes."

"You will come after I've teased your body to the proper level, Moira. I want you to scream it. I want you to drown in it. Are you willing to give yourself over to me completely?"

She licked her lips, trying to concentrate on his words while he thrust his fingers in and out and stroked every once in a while over her swollen clit. "Yes."

"Good," he purred. "I will only bring you pleasure in the bedroom, Moira. This, I promise."

He removed his fingers from her passage and swept his tongue down over her, drawing her labia into his warm mouth and sucking at them gently. His tongue played with the entrance of her passage, then thrust within it. He groaned. "You are as sweet as I thought you'd be." He slid his tongue back inside her over and over, as though it was his shaft. Moira gasped and bucked on the bed. He grasped her hips, holding her in place. "Sweet and hot and tight," he said when he'd stopped. "I can't wait to slide my cock into you."

He stroked his finger down to play with her anus. No man had ever touched her there before. She jerked and he shushed her. "Remember our agreement, Moira. You said *all* and gave your body into my care. I intend to give you the full treatment."

Dain stroked over it again while he speared his tongue into her pussy. He did it as though gentling her to his touch. Nerves she hadn't even known she'd possessed sprang to life and she let out a low moan. Goddess help her, she liked it. She liked it all. She loved the way he commanded her in bed and how he touched her.

"Ah, yes, you enjoy my way of loving," he murmured against her labia when she moaned. "I thought you might, Moira. I suspected a wanton desire within you. Ah, it's the loveliest thing," he groaned. "I can't get enough of the taste of you." He went back to alternatively teasing her clit with the tip of his tongue and drawing her labia into the recesses of his mouth.

Moira let out a strangled cry and her body tensed. She wanted him to slide his phallus inside her and slam into her. She wanted to hear the slap of his skin against hers. She wanted to feel him possess her and lose control to her at the same time.

"God...Moira. Turn over. On your hand and knees." His voice shook.

"Dain?"

"Moira," he said gutturally. "Do as I tell you. You won't be sorry." He lifted up, allowing her to move.

She rose up and turned over. She felt the slide of his hand over her buttocks and she closed her eyes, resting her cheek against the cool comforter on the bed. Moira could barely feel the cold of the room now. Dain had heated her body to a fever pitch.

He inserted two fingers into her passage once more, this time from behind. He did not thrust, but let his fingers simply stretch and fill her. "Spread your thighs farther, beautiful," he asked of her.

She spread her legs and that gave him room to rub her clit with his other hand. Fingers of pleasure shot up her spine and throughout her body. It made her want more, want completion. "Yes, please," she sobbed out through a constricted throat. "Please, make me come, Dain. No more torture."

He thrust his fingers in and out, and at the same time took her clit between two fingers and rubbed the small bundle of sensitized nerves back and forth. Her climax came hard and fast. It crashed over her in an explosion and she cried out from the force of it. Waves of pleasure washed through her, stealing her breath and making her gasp. Her muscles clenched and released around his fingers and she felt the liquid of her passage flow out of her. The spasms racking her passage made her vision go black and she nearly passed out from the force of it.

"Yes, Moira. That's it," Dain purred from behind her. "You don't know how pretty you are when you're unrestrained this way."

She collapsed onto the bed and twisted to lie on her back. She was sheened with perspiration, despite the chill air. Her breath came fast. "Now you, Dain. I want you. Please." She spread her thighs, exposing her pussy. She was still aroused despite her climax.

He knelt down and buried his face between her thighs, lapping up all her cream. Mora gasped at the feel of his greedy tongue licking over her labia and her clit. He made a small sound, like she was the best thing he'd ever tasted, and

Moira gasped and clenched the comforter in both hands under his ravenous onslaught.

"Please," she sobbed. Another climax tensed her body and when Dain closed his mouth over her clit and sucked on it, it rushed forward and overwhelmed her.

"Ah, yes," Dain hissed. When the spasms of her climax still racked her, he spread her thighs wide and slid the head of his cock into her pussy.

"Dain!" she cried. He slid in an inch, then withdrew and slid in a bit farther. Sweat broke out on his forehead as he apparently endeavored not to injure her with his length. Inch by inch she took him. He stretched her like she'd never been stretched, filling every bit of her. She gasped and then moaned deeply at the exquisite pleasure of it.

"Your sex is so slick, sweet, and tight," he bit off. He pulled out nearly all the way and took her by her hips. In one smooth, hard surge, he sheathed himself inside her to the hilt. She cried out as the spasms racked her a third time. The muscles of her pussy pulsed and squeezed around his shaft like a ravenous mouth consuming him. Dain threw back his head and groaned low and deep. Then he began to move.

Moira saw stars as the thick, ridged length of him moved piston-like in and out of her. He held her by her waist, and his hips hit her inner thighs with every inward stroke, making a slapping sound of flesh on flesh. She grabbed the blankets and held on when he took her pussy hard and fast, over and over. The head of his cock brushed over some sensitive spot deep within her with every inward stroke, making her sob and cry with the pleasure of it.

She moaned wantonly, uncaring of anyone who might be able to hear her. Her fingers clenched and released the bedcovers and she spread her knees even farther apart, giving him complete access and free rein over her. He stared down at her, his gaze intense. For a moment they locked gazes. Moira felt a quickening of sorts between them, a touching of her soul against his. Dain's eyes widened and he averted his gaze. Moira's happiness diminished in that moment, but soon she didn't think of it anymore...didn't think of anything anymore. Dain grabbed her hips and increased the pace and power of his thrusts with a single-minded purpose that took Moira's breath away. His cock rubbed her pleasure point deep within. With every thrust he stroked it exactly right. It reduced her to a panting, moaning bundle of need.

He reached forward and took a breast in each hand, kneading and massaging. He tweaked the nipples between his fingertips. Her next climax hit her hard. She sucked in a breath and let it out in a cry. The muscles of her core milked his cock.

Dain called her name and she felt him explode within her, his shaft pulsing as it released its seed to bathe her womb. He collapsed down beside her. His breathing was harsh in her ears. He pulled her close and brushed his lips across her temple. "You'll be the death of me, woman," he murmured. "I want more of you."

They made love again, slower this time, then again once more after that. Never did he risk looking into her eyes again. He seemed unwilling to risk the kind of connection they'd shared for a moment before. It was only right before dawn that they tumbled down onto the mattress for the final time, intertwined their limbs, and fell asleep.

When Moira woke hours later her body was deliciously sore and she felt languorously relaxed. She found Dain had tucked her under the heavy blankets of the bed and fed the fire so that it now blazed instead of sputtered.

But Dain was gone.

* * * * *

Moira didn't see Dain during the two weeks that followed. He was like a ghost. Less substantial than a ghost, really, since the castle ghosts all made her quite aware of their presence. He simply disappeared, much as he'd done for the first month she'd been here.

Killian kept her company, playing chess with her from time to time. Once in a while, she felt Dain as he watched them from the shadows. Once in a while she scented his spicy soap scent in the air he'd just occupied when she turned a corner, or opened a door. He watched her from the shadows, but never sought her out.

She thought of trying to find his bedchambers, of finding some excuse to inquire it of Killian or Bess, but decided against it. Dain was a man who needed careful handling. If he didn't want to see her, then she wouldn't seek him out, either.

Though the memory of his hands on her still made her shiver with longing in the deep of night. She'd searched all her pillows and bedding for his scent for days after their night together. Dain had made her body sing in a way no other man ever had. He had brought her easily, over and over that night. He had brought her so many times that she'd been left limp, listless, relaxed and extremely content.

Dain was dominant in bed, single-minded and almost ruthless in his style of loving. It suited Moira in a way she never would've imagined had he not shown it to her. It made her body hungry for more of him, while her heart and mind thirsted for his presence…for his regard. Something he was denying her.

Moira closed the door of her room and headed downstairs to breakfast. Outside, the snow still fell. She glanced out a window as she passed by and sighed. She was getting nowhere here. She was nowhere closer to finding an explanation for her psychic fits than she was when she had first arrived. What she really needed was a cure for them.

She stopped in the middle of the corridor and stared out one of the floor-to-ceiling windows. When the snow melted away enough for her mount to make the trip, she would leave this strange place and the compelling Dain. It was clear he did not want her friendship or companionship. It was clear she did not hold the same fascination for him that he held for her.

Something around her heart squeezed. Dain was lost to the world. That was a sorrowful thing, but true. He was lost forever to the events of the past, to his own dark, inner demons. It was already too late for him. She would do far better to forget a man such as he.

She gave her head a small shake. At the first possible time she could leave, she would take her mount and head southward, through the pass of Anthrum to the Port of Paradise. Her instincts told her to head to the governing city, and so she would. Clearly, she needed to locate Cyric in order to make headway in this mystery.

Dain was of no help to her.

She stiffened, sensing him before he touched her. "What do you want?" she asked in a flat tone.

Behind her, Dain hesitated, and then stepped forward. "How did you know it was me?"

She glanced at him and shrugged. "I have an aptitude for sensing ghosts, and that is mostly what you are."

He winced, as though she'd struck him and she felt bad...for a moment. Her feelings were a bit piqued that he'd made mind-numbing love to her over and over that night and had then spent two weeks avoiding her.

"It was your scent as well," she continued. "You and Killian use different soaps and therefore each have your own distinctive scent."

"You are angry," he said.

She shrugged again. "I have no reason to be pleased."

"What is it you want from me?" he asked softly.

She paused a moment, then turned to face him. She put all the emotion she felt at that moment into her eyes, all her anger and longing and, yes, hope. "More," she answered steadily.

He moved so quickly that she barely had time to draw a breath. He caught her up in his arms and kissed her. His lips slid over hers like hot silk, tasting and taking at the same time. He coaxed her mouth open with a small flutter of his tongue against her lips and she tightened her fingers around his upper arms and held on under the erotic onslaught of his tongue sliding in and mating with hers. A small sound of yearning escaped her throat before she could swallow it down.

"Why do you want me?" Dain murmured against her lips in between kisses. "What insanity fills you that you would ask for *more* of me?"

"I have been asking myself that very same question," she answered, "but I cannot deny that you are very…compelling to me."

He walked her back a couple paces and turned her to face the wall. His breathing was harsh and sweet against her ear. "Compelling? What do you mean by compelling?" He let his hands roam over her waist, and then higher, smoothing over the bodice of her dress and her breasts within it. The feel of his large, warm hands on her and the remembrance of what they could do to her made her breath catch in her throat.

"It means, um, something complicated," she gasped as he ran his fingertips over her taut nipples. "Something deep and intimate. I don't really understand it, myself."

He plucked at her nipples through the material of her gown, drawing a low moan from her. "Does it mean you want me, Moira, my sweet?" he rasped in her ear. "Does it mean you want me in your bed...or perhaps that you wish me to ask you into mine? Or maybe you'd prefer me to *order* you to my bed, and request of you the same level of trust during our previous tryst? I think that would excite you."

Her pussy responded to his words as though he'd primed her by his own hand. Her clit grew swollen and sensitive. Her pussy readied itself for sex.

He reached down and gathered her skirt in one hand, drawing it upward toward her waist. "Is that what you want, Moira?"

"Yes," she hissed. "Sweet Goddess, yes."

His fingertips grazed her stomach, dipped lower to brush over her mound through her undergarment. He groaned low in his throat. "So eager. Eagerness becomes you." He slipped his hand down the front of her panties. "Is this more of what you want?" He rubbed over her clit and slipped down to slide his middle finger into her heat.

Moira grasped the edge of the window with one hand and splayed the other out flat against the wall. A hard, fast breath hissed out between her lips.

Dain thrust his finger in and out very slowly, over and over and over. He drew her moisture out as she soaked his hand in her desire. Her pussy felt sensitive, hot and slippery with her cream.

"Ah, Moira," he said in a rough voice. "I've been dreaming of doing this since the night we spent together. There nothing in this world that feels better than you. I've thought about taking you again every single hour of every single day since we last parted."

"Then why have you stayed away?" Her words came slowly since the pleasure Dain gave her body seemed to dull most of her cognitive ability.

The slide of his finger into her body stopped for a moment, but he didn't answer her. "Turn around," he said roughly as he pulled his hand from her underwear.

She turned. He caught her under her chin and kissed her hard. At the same time, he slid her undergarment down and off. Her hands went to the waistband of his trews and she freed the buttons and pushed them down to stroke his rigid and ready cock. Just the sight of it made her even wetter between the thighs.

They both fumbled raising her skirts. She hooked one leg around his waist as he guided his cock into her and pushed in. "Ah, yes, Dain," she moaned in a sensation that was near relief at the feel of him filling and stretching her to the maximum limit. It was like she'd been missing a part of herself she'd forgotten about.

Dain splayed a hand flat against the wall beside her head and hissed out a breath. He closed his eyes as though in ecstasy. He opened his eyes and stared straight down into hers. "You are paradise," he murmured.

He kept his gaze locked with hers as he started to move. The insistence of his gaze on hers made the act deeper and more pleasurable, more intimate. This time he didn't look away when their gazes locked and that same soul-deep sensation of connection flared between them. He let her see everything this time. Her lips parted and her breath caught as she examined the depth and breadth of the pain within him. Her hands sought and found fistfuls of his shirt and she moved her hips downward, matching his thrusts and trying to get him ever deeper within her body, as if trying to take a little of that burden from him and absorb it into herself.

Finally, the pain in his eyes flared and he broke the connection.

Dain kept the pace slow, so slow and easy that it sent little shivers of pleasure throughout her body. Finally, she closed her eyes and came long and hard. She felt her muscles clench and release around his length and her cream spill out of her, soaking his cock and running down her inner thighs.

When the last spasm had racked her, Dain cupped her bottom in his hands and quickened the pace. He pushed up and in, thrusting faster and harder into the depths of her. At the same time, he let one hand stray back and play with her nether hole. She started in surprise, but relaxed as she realized she had a thousand little nerve endings there she never knew would feel so good when stimulated. Dain seemed to know just how to play each of them. "Dain," she gasped in surprise.

"Do you like that?" he growled into her ear.

"Goddess, yes," she moaned.

He slipped a finger into the small, tight opening and thrust it in and out. Moria's hips bucked forward as a climax flirted hard with her body. She dug her fingers into his upper arms for support.

"Some women like it when a man takes her here," he murmured.

"Uhn," was all she could say in response.

"Some women like it when both places are stimulated at the same time. Some women like it when two men take them at once. One cock for each place. I saw you with my brother that day."

She went stiff in his arms.

"Have you been with him yet?"

She shook her head.

"You want to be, though. I can tell." He leaned down and caught her earlobe between his teeth, gently pulling at it and she relaxed. "I think you'd like two men at once, Moira. I can just imagine how excited you'd be. Tell me. Would you like that?"

"Y-yes, maybe," she breathed.

He added one more finger to the first and thrust gently in and out. It was just a little pain...*just enough.*

Moira screamed as her climax hit her full force, this one stronger than the last.

This time, her orgasm fed his. Dain thrust deeply within her and she felt his cock jump. He groaned low near her ear as he shot his come into her. Then, as the last tremors left them both, he whispered, "Moira," and withdrew.

Her skirts fell back into place, but a part of her regretted the loss of him. He felt so good when he was connected to her.

Dain turned away and she caught his arm, forcing him to turn back to her. "You will not do that to me again," she said. "I will not allow you to come to me, make love to me and then leave." Her voice was like steel. She instantly regretted the words *make love*, but there they were. To her, it felt that way.

Emotions passed like quickly moving clouds over his face — surprise, hope...and sorrow. He shook his head. "You want more from me, but I don't how to give it. Do you understand? I don't know how. I can give you sex, Moira, nothing more."

She said nothing, her joy at their union fading at his words and the look in his eyes.

He leaned forward, brushed a tendril of her escaped hair back away from her face, and kissed her tenderly. "My chamber is on the fourth floor of the north tower. Come there whenever you wish." His voice hardened and he smoothed his hand over her cheek. "But when you enter, know that you are in my domain. You must trust me there, my sweet Moira, and allow me whatever I may wish…within reason."

She licked her lips. "All right." She would take what she could get of him.

He nodded. "All right."

* * * * *

Moira fingered a chess piece, fitting her thumb into the graceful carving on its side. The expression on Dain's face and in his eyes during their encounter in the hall was all she could see in her imagination. He was like he wanted her but feared her in the same breath. She didn't have to wonder where the fear was, but Moira wondered if he could overcome it. Sometimes she thought that perhaps he could, perhaps there was the tiniest chance he might overcome the past, and other times she deemed it completely hopeless.

"Moira?"

She lifted her head at the sound of Killian's voice. He looked concerned.

"It's your move."

"I'm sorry," she murmured. She frowned at the board for a moment, thinking, and made her move.

Killian checkmated her. He set her piece to the side and stared at her. "Are you all right? You seem distracted."

Moira ran a hand through her hair nervously. "Honestly? I think of your brother. Is he never to know happiness again?"

Killian leaned forward. "Not if he has anything to say about it. Dain doesn't think he deserves happiness. Moira…" He trailed off and sighed.

"Yes?"

He shifted in his seat. "If Dain pushes you away, don't take it to heart."

She smiled. "I understand Dain's situation, Killian, believe me. Thank you for being concerned for my welf—" In that moment pain overwhelmed her, filling up every part of her world. She gasped and collapsed to her knees next to the table, grabbing the edge of the board and spilling the pieces to the floor. Blinding, white-hot bolts shot through her head.

"Moira!" cried Killian. "Dain, Bess, come now!" he yelled as he dropped to his knees beside her.

She pressed her palm to her forehead, trying ineffectually to drive away the agony. She cringed away from the firelight, even that hurt.

She heard pounding footsteps, two male voices...then knew nothing.

Chapter Six

&

Moira woke to the sound of two low male voices. Her eyelids fluttered open, but she closed them again against the light coming in through the window. Her head pounded so badly, it nearly drowned out the sound of Dain and Killian who were in deep discussion near the foot of her bed.

"I thought you didn't want to find Cyric," said Killian.

Through her barely slitted eyes, she saw Dain flick a glance at her. "I don't, but this has to stop."

The note of concern in his voice made something pleasant and warm bloom in the center of her chest. It almost completely chased away the pain of her head. That had been the worst attack since the one that had driven her to seek Dain out.

"You're starting to care for her," came Killian's pleased voice.

Dain said nothing in response.

Feeling like she was eavesdropping, she allowed her eyelids to flutter open a bit. "The window," she croaked. "The light."

Heavy, masculine footsteps crossed the floor and Moira heard the rustling sound of the curtains being closed.

A large hand covered her forehead and the touch seemed to draw the pain from her skull. She opened her eyes to find Dain looking down at her with worry in his eyes. She tried to smile at him, but it was really more of a grimace.

"That was a bad one," he murmured. "I'm relieved to see you awake. Did you see anything?"

Wincing, she pushed herself up a bit in the bed. She shook her head. "No," she rasped, then cleared her throat. "There was just pain."

Dain stood staring at her for a moment, and then he turned away and walked to the window, rubbing a hand over his face. "They have to stop," he said almost to himself.

Killian brought her a glass of water that she drank gratefully. "I don't even know what this has to do with you, Dain. Maybe nothing," she said. She shook her head. "I would never request that you have a confrontation with your greatest enemy on my account."

He turned to face her. "Why wouldn't you ask this?"

She shrugged. "You and I have no real tie. It isn't my place to ask something so large of you. This is my battle, not yours."

Dain walked toward her slowly, his face seemed to smolder with emotion and unsaid things. He stopped beside her and laid his palm to her cheek. "You truly think we have no ties?"

She looked away. He was too damaged for her to hope for anything beyond a carnal relation. He'd said it himself in the corridor. It would not do to dissemble, not with such heavy, emotional issues. Better they kept their relationship as it was, kept it honest. It was physical and nothing more. It was no matter that she might pine for more than that in her heart.

"A few days ago in the corridor we were connected," he said softly and then walked slowly out of the room and closed the door behind him.

She took another drink of water, her hand shaking just a little.

Killian had watched the whole incident carefully. He stepped forward and took the glass from her. "Are you hungry? Bess would be more than happy to prepare something for you."

She shook her head gently and reached out a hand with a smile. "Sit with me a little, will you, Killian?" Her desire was completely genuine. She enjoyed Killian's company very much. There was a quality that Killian possessed that drew her to him. It was unlike what she felt for Dain. She felt friendliness and deep affection for Killian...and yes, physical attraction, but it wasn't the burning, passionate attraction as she had for Dain.

Dain she could love deeply, passionately and with all her heart.

Killian she could marry and have a nice, even relationship with.

Killian sat down on a chair near her bedside and took her hand. The only reason she even had that particular thought was she knew that Killian was drawn to her in a romantic way. Not only could she feel it with her extrasensory abilities, but she could see it glimmering in the depths of his eyes. Killian was always assessing her on a carnal level.

"I know," started Killian carefully, "what has been going between you and my brother. Why do you push him away?"

She looked down and picked at the blue woolen blanket that covered her. "It is an impossible thing that lies between Dain and myself. He is far too damaged for me to ever hope he might think of a true relationship with me."

Killian rubbed his thumb over her palm and made her shiver. His touch was much as his brother's. "He was very concerned when you fainted," he said quietly.

"Was he?" she answered lightly.

"He was agitated and barking orders at everyone." Killian smiled. "Yes, he was worried."

She sighed. "Your brother is a complex man."

"I was also concerned."

She smiled and squeezed his hand. "I'll be fine."

"My brother's feelings for you go deeper than you both know. I can see it, but I think I'm the only one who can."

She shrugged and looked away.

Killian took her hand in his and guided her chin back to look at him. "I want to help you make him see. I want to help bring the two of you closer."

Moira closed her eyes briefly. She wanted that too, but… "He's too far gone, Killian—"

"No! Don't even think of giving up on him, Moira. You may be his only way back to the light."

A part of her flared with hope at his words. Maybe Killian was right, maybe it wasn't too late.

But the haunted look in Dain's eyes when he'd taken her in the corridor said differently.

He guided her gaze to him. "But know this, Moira, if Dain is indeed too damaged to love again, *I* want you."

Her eyes widened.

"I know you don't love me as you love Dain, but you and I could have a good marriage, a marriage built on strong friendship and respect. Do you understand?"

She nodded. Had she not been thinking that very thing?

He kissed her cheek tenderly. "Just remember what I've said."

* * * * *

Dain resisted the urge to punch the stone wall in his chambers. Why had her words pricked him? Not only had they pricked…they'd punched. She wanted him for sex and nothing more. For some reason, that knowledge hurt him.

Even though he'd said as much in the corridor, the look in her eyes and the sentiment coming from her lips had nearly been more than he could bear.

She believed him capable of giving her no more emotion than what was required during the carnal act. She was right, but that did not stop a part of him deep inside from yearning for the ability to give her more. He wanted to love her, care for her, protect her, but he could do none of these things. Not while the chaotic, violent magick he possessed thrummed through his veins.

All the same, he couldn't deny the fact he regretted her feelings…and his own. He wished he didn't care that she thought they had no connection beyond a physical one, but the woman had touched him deeply.

She'd managed to get under his skin and stay there. Now he was failing to imagine life without her presence in his castle. Without the sweet scent of her wafting through the air, down a corridor he passed through after she'd occupied it. Without her laughter ringing through a distant room as Killian or Bess amused her.

Had he ever made her laugh?

He shook his head and paced to the opposite end of his chamber. No. He'd only made her moan, scream, claw the sheets. He was incapable of making her laugh.

Perhaps, in the end, he was unfit for her.

Still, she occupied his every thought these days. He dreamed of her at night and had to force himself to not get up and go to her. As he fell asleep, it was to the image of her nude and cloaked only in velvet shadows and his own broad hands. He wanted the scent of her body rubbed against his own as if in marking. He wanted it in his blankets, on his pillows, so that when he awoke in the morning, it was to the smell of her.

He paced to the fireplace and rested a hand against the wide mantel. The heat rose up and hit him in the face. He closed his eyes and sighed. She haunted him, totally and completely. It had made him nearly forget one very important part. Dain opened his eyes and stared into the fire.

The rage he felt that day when he came home and found Andreea with Cyric was still within him. The dark magick that had shattered the windows, the pottery and the glass and killed his wife was still in him.

He couldn't risk exposing Moira to that. He couldn't risk endangering her that way. It was completely selfish of him. He had to think of her safety. With him, she had none.

With his brother, she would have some.

As much as it pained him to think of the two of them together, the idea that Moira might find happiness…love with Killian overrode his feelings of jealousy. He only wanted both their happiness. Perhaps they could find that together.

* * * * *

A week later, the sun came out and the snow began to melt. Moira stood from where she'd been sitting and reading by the fire. She was now fully recovered from her last attack and luckily hadn't had any more. She walked over and pulled the drapes of her bedroom window open to watch the relentless drip, drip of the melting icicles that hung from the castle eaves.

She viewed the sight with mixed emotions. Soon, she would be able to travel to the Port of Paradise, to search for Cyric. Maybe if she located him, he would be able to shed light on the mystery of these psychic attacks.

But that would also mean leaving Dain.

It was twilight now and the sun was descending behind a snow-covered mountain in the distance, mixing the sky through with a blend of reds, oranges, yellows and purples. The intricate shading of color felt as complex as her own heart. Soon she would leave this place and who knew if she'd ever return?

She watched as the sun dipped lower and lower, bleeding all the colors from the sky. In the east, the full moon rose, reflecting its pale, silvery light off the snow.

Craving the feel of Dain's body against hers, she unbound the heavy fall of her hair from the tight knot at her nape. Dain loved her hair loose. Then she turned and left the room. When she reached Dain's chamber, the door was ajar almost as if he'd been expecting her. Firelight flickered out into the cold corridor, licking at the stone walls in an inviting way.

Soundlessly, she pushed the door open a little farther and entered his chamber. Dain sat propped up on his large four-poster bed with his eyes closed. He was shirtless and shoeless and the light licked over the muscled plane of his chest. He should have been cold, but the temperature never seemed to bother him.

On silent feet, she went toward him as if drawn by an unseen force. As she went, she toed off her slippers and discarded her heavy winter wrap. Once at his bedside, she reached out and laid her hand on his chest, just above his heart.

His eyes popped open. In the same moment, he grabbed her wrist and he tumbled her to the bed and covered her body with his. "Hello," he said softly.

Fighting to get her breath back, she smiled. "Hello." The pressure of his body on hers felt delicious. She wanted more contact.

He kneed her thighs apart and pressed his already hard cock against her. "You came," he murmured, then dipped his head and kissed her. "I've been dreaming you would."

"I tried to stay away."

"Why?"

Instead of answering, she pushed up. He allowed her to push him over onto his back. Hiking her skirts, she climbed on him and started undoing his trews, while she kissed his lips, throat and chest in abandon. She finally got her hand down his pants and stroked his hard length from crown to base. Dain groaned low and long.

She blinked and found herself flat on her back again. "You didn't answer my question," he said as he lifted her skirt and drew his hand very slowly up her calf to her inner knee to her outer thigh. "Answer it."

Her breath came faster as his fingers found her undergarment and ripped it. "Dain!" she gasped.

"You don't need it," he answered her silkily. "Now, answer."

"I-I'll be leaving soon."

He paused. "Ah. Well, that is a pity." Dain backed up and went to a shadowy corner of his room. When he came back, it was with several long strips of material in his hand. He set them on the bed and stripped off his half-unbuttoned trews. "Maybe I'll just have to tie you down to ensure you stay a bit longer."

Her heart went pitter-patter at a slightly faster rate. "Tie me up?"

He lifted his brow in response.

Her gaze flew to the ties that lay on the bed.

He leaned forward, one hand on each side of her and kissed her. "Nervous?" he asked as he pulled away. "You trust me, don't you?"

She stared into his eyes, her lips parted, and nodded. "I told you that I do."

He grasped her gown and pulled it over her head. The dress ended up draped over a nearby chair. His gaze roved her nude body. She should've been cold, but the look in his eyes warmed her all the way through.

Dain leaned over her, wrapping one arm around her waist, and kissed her until she lost her breath. "All I want is to have you here in my bed, bound and at my mercy," he purred.

Moira shivered at his words. He could do anything to her he wanted. Her body was already responding to him and he'd barely touched her.

He pulled her up so she lay in the center of his bed. Then he removed the pillows and positioned her flat on her back. Dain took the ties and, with his gaze ever fixed on her, tied her wrists, leaving her legs free.

He leaned back, admiring his handiwork. "You are the most beautiful woman I have ever seen, Moira."

She shifted her legs and felt her cheeks flush at his praise.

He dipped his hand down between her thighs and felt how wet she was for him. When he toyed with her clit, she let out a low moan.

"You're very excited by this," he murmured in a pleased tone. "Remember in the corridor, Moira? What I said about my brother?"

She bit her lip and whimpered at the slide of the pad of his finger that leisurely stroked her clit. "Yes," she finally gasped.

"I'm going to invite him now. You'll like it. You'll like having four hands on you and two mouths. You'll like having two cocks ready to pleasure you."

He stroked a finger through her folds, gathering moisture, so he could better tease her clit. Images of both Dain and Killian taking her filled her mind. Having both their cocks to kiss and touch. Having them both filling her... The fantasies flitted through her mind as Dain worked her clit back and forth. She cried out as she came, soaking his hand.

Dain chuckled as he brushed his fingers through her damp curls. "I think you like the idea."

She trembled against the waves that still racked her body and nodded. That, she couldn't deny. The thought of having Dain and Killian both at once excited her more than she ever thought it would, fueling her desire to a fever pitch.

He backed away and covered her with a blanket. Then he left. When he returned, it was with his brother. Her gaze sought and held Killian's and she twisted against the ties, feeling the delicious scrape of the material against her skin.

"Now there's a sight to stop a man's heart," Killian said as he entered the room. His gaze ate her up from head to foot as he approached the bed. It made Moira's breath come faster.

Dain slid in beside her and kissed her as he drew the blanket slowly away from her nude body. Killian groaned. She grew wet between her thighs at the sound and her nipples hardened.

Dain knelt on one side of her and traced his hands over her body, massaging and rubbing out the tenseness in her muscles. She shuddered every time his broad palms passed over her breasts or inner thighs.

As Dain rubbed the tender, sensitive flesh at the backs of her knees, Killian lowered himself down into the bed beside her and placed his hand on her stomach. "I have dreamed of this," he murmured. "But are you sure?"

She bit her lip and nodded. She cared for both these men. She trusted both of them. Since she would be leaving soon, she wanted both of them.

Killian stood and drew his clothing off. She watched each article disappear, revealing a beautiful body that was much like Dain's. Though Killian had fewer battle scars marking his flesh...he had fewer scars both inside and out. He stood nude before her, his gaze dark and intent on her face, as he passed a hand over his impressive erection.

Dain also unclothed and she turned her attention to him as Killian sank down to her on the bed. Soon both men were gloriously naked and kneeling on either side of her, both willing...and wanting...to give her their sole attention. That knowledge was almost enough to make Moira climax on the spot.

Killian rubbed his thumb over the smooth skin of her stomach, drawing little circles higher and higher. Every pass of his finger made her body burn hotter. Finally, he reached her breast and closed his hand around it, teasing the nipple with his thumb. At the same time, he leaned in and tasted her lips, their first kiss.

Killian's kiss was less urgent than Dain's. It was sweeter and nicer and arousing, but it did not fire her blood the way Dain's kiss did. It didn't make her weak in the knees, fluttery in her chest. His tongue stole in and brushed against hers, sending ripples of pleasure up her spine. It still had the capability to arouse her, however. She moaned into his mouth and he deepened the kiss, driving his tongue more aggressively against hers.

Dain leaned down and took her other nipple in his mouth and she arched her back, gasping into Killian's mouth. Killian smiled against her lips at her reaction and dropped down to lick the nipple he'd been caressing.

Moira grabbed the ties that bound her and closed her eyes at the sensation of both their dark heads bent over her breasts, and the feel of their tongues and lips nipping and teasing and laving over her aching nipples.

In tandem, with the practiced ease of men who'd taken more than one woman at the same time, they eased their hands down over her belly to her pussy. She spread her thighs for them in welcome and lost track of who touched where. All that was left was a sea of almost overwhelming sensation. One stroked her clit relentlessly, making her writhe and moan. The other rubbed his fingers along her sensitive opening, then breached it and thrust inside her. He found her sweet spot and rasped his fingertip over it and over it with a masterfulness that brought her right to the edge of climax.

Then both of them were there, each with a finger buried deep within her. Together, in tandem, they stroked in and out of her.

Killian broke away with a gasp. "So silky and hot," he groaned.

Moira grabbed the ties as her hips bucked forward. She whimpered as her climax rose, wanting more, wanting their cocks. Finally, she screamed out her orgasm, digging her heels into the bed with her legs as far apart as she could get them.

They gentled her down easily with murmurings and small strokes. When they'd finally passed she drew in a shuddering breath. "Release me," she murmured. "I need to touch you both."

Dain reached up and undid her bonds, and she slid into his arms, kissing him, running her hands over his upper arms and back and tangling her fingers through his hair. She felt wild for the feel of him and couldn't get enough fast enough. He crushed her to him, rubbing the length of his body against her and drinking at her mouth and tongue as though he was parched.

Behind her, Killian braced himself against her back, sliding his hard chest along her skin. His hands traced over her thighs, her hips and finally up to cup her breasts. In front, she felt Dain's hard cock pressing against her.

Moira fought a decadent purr rising up from her throat. She moaned into Dain's mouth. Her pleasure centers were high at the feel of these two men bracing her front and back. She had never felt so warm, so safe, so excited.

Moira turned in Dain's arms to face Killian. She didn't feel for him the same way she felt for Dain, but he was still a man she kept deeply and preciously in her heart. He was a man she would never forget and always think of in caring and fondness, if not love. She caught his gaze and his pupils dilated, giving away his arousal. She leaned in and kissed his lips softly. It wasn't enough for him. He crushed his mouth to hers and kissed her back with ravenous hunger, sliding his hand back to cup the nape of her neck. When she parted her lips for him, he slid his tongue within and mated it with hers.

Behind her, Dain kissed his way along her shoulder and back. He ran his lips sensually over her buttocks and kissed the back of her thighs. Everywhere his mouth touched, fire trailed.

Killian pressed her down onto the bed, even as her hands sought his cock. His breath hissed out of him as her fingers closed around his rigid length and pumped. He was the same size as Dain, almost.

Dain eased her thighs apart and settled between them. He parted her labia and examined her. She felt a drop of cream pearl on the entrance of her pussy and drip down her inner thigh. With a deep groan, Dain licked it up. Moira gasped and Killian covered her mouth with his, eating up all the little moans and noises she made as Dain started licking her. His broad, flat tongue felt like heaven. Her clit became immediately needy once more under the feel of it.

Dain was relentless in the attention he gave to her sex. It made Moira's heart beat faster and her breathing hitch in her throat. It skated her right to the razor's edge of a climax, but he held her there, not allowing her to come. She moved her hips restlessly, knowing he did it on purpose, knowing it would do her no good to beg him. He meant to drive her deeper into ecstasy and increase the power of her climax once it finally came.

"Killian," she gasped. "Let me taste you. I need to have you in my mouth."

He rose up and straddled her, presenting his thick, wide cock to her lips.

She grasped him at the wide base of his shaft and fondled his balls.

"Ah, Anot, yes," he hissed above her. "I wanted this so much before."

Closing her eyes in anticipation, she licked the head, feeling the smoothness of the crown. She dragged her tongue around it and stroked downward along the shaft.

Between her thighs, Dain grasped her inner thighs, holding them apart and pinned them to the bed as he coaxed her clit from its hood with small little licks of his tongue, causing her to stop and gasp. Dain made a low noise in his throat as she shuddered against him in pleasure. He licked her from her anus to her clit over and over until she threw back her head from Killian's cock and keened.

Realizing she was neglecting Killian, she tipped her head forward and engulfed his cock between her lips. Killian groaned and arched his back, sliding his cock farther into her mouth. She suckled him, moving her lips up and down his length. Moira allowed her tongue to stroke up and down his shaft, playing especially with the small knot of nerves just below the crown where she knew a man was most sensitive.

Dain slid his tongue into her pussy, causing her hips to thrust forward. He toyed with her nether hole idly with his finger, stroking it and circling it. All the tiny nerves there flared to glorious life. She moaned around Killian's length and squeezed her eyes shut. Killian grabbed onto the headboard above her and groaned out his pleasure as she suckled him faster and harder, in accord with the rising pleasure between her thighs.

Dain pulled away. "Enough," he gasped. "I must have her."

Killian nodded and pulled away. His cock looked unbearably hard, but she would ease him. She knew Dain meant for her to ease them both. Killian moved to the side, revealing Dain. He stared at her with a single-minded intensity that made her already throbbing clit pulse even harder. He reached over and took something from the table by the bed, the vial he'd placed there when he'd gone to get the ties. "Come here," he murmured.

She got up and crawled across the bed toward him. Her long, thick hair hung like two curtains across her face. Crawling the way she was she must've looked as wild and as wanton as she felt. When she reached him, Dain curled a hand to the back of her head, dragging her up against him, and kissed her long and hard. Moira could taste herself on his tongue. It made her curl her fingers around his shoulders and hang on for dear life at the eroticism. He had her panting when he was through. Dain pulled her down, so she lay stomach down in his lap.

Killian moved in to sit nearby. He reached out and rubbed her buttocks. Her pussy felt like it was on fire. It was reddened and wet and plumped like ripened fruit. She had to fight not to raise her hips and spread her thighs, had to fight not to beg Killian to touch her, finish her off. All she could do was whimper.

"Killian, a pillow," said Dain.

She turned her face to the side and saw Killian reach for a pillow. Dain put it under her, so it lifted her rear into the air a little. Apparently, Killian knew what was to come. She did not. She lifted up a little in sudden apprehension and Dain pressed her back down.

"Remember what I said in the corridor, Moira? If you enter this room, you're mine to do with as I please. Give this a chance. If you don't enjoy it, I will go no further. You've only to say," he said. "I would never do anything that didn't cause you pleasure."

She relaxed and settled back down again. Killian reached over and smoothed her hair away from her face, then ran his fingers down to massage the nape of her neck. Dain started at her feet, gently rubbing away the small tension she felt at the unknown. Killian worked down, running his hands down to the small of her back and finally to her buttocks. Dain reached her upper thighs and told her to part her legs. She did so and he ran his fingertips up her sex in a teasing way that made her bite her lower lip.

Killian traced over the mound of her buttocks and ran his finger over the crease. In his other hand, he grasped his own length. With her head turned to the side, she watched, fascinated, as he stroked himself. She wished she could taste him again, but sensed they had other plans at the moment. Killian and Dain both ran their fingers over the heart of her and Moira hissed out a breath and grasped fistfuls of the blanket.

"It will get better, love," purred Killian. "We must make you ready to take us."

She let out a strangled, tormented little laugh. "You sound like you've done this before."

Killian dragged his fingertips over her aroused flesh. "This is Nordan, of course we have."

Dain reached over and took the vial he'd laid on the bed. He squeezed some oil onto Killian's hand and then onto his own. "What's that?" she asked.

Dain lowered his fingers to her sex and rubbed the oil into her clit and labia. It was slippery, seemed warm and made her gasp in pleasure. "This is an ointment people use to make sex easier. Don't worry, I would never do anything to hurt you." He snapped his mouth shut on the end of that sentence, as if realizing what he'd said. Moira held her breath for a moment, willing the past to go away, if just for a little while. "Just relax. Stay open for us," he finished in a terse voice.

She had little time to consider his words, for Killian dipped his hand down and rubbed the oil over her nether entrance. Moira moaned. "Do you like that, love?" asked Killian.

She closed her eyes and nodded.

"You'll like this better, then," he murmured as he breached her anus with the tip of a finger.

She gasped at the sensation. It felt better than she ever would've imagined. He thrust in and out gently, slowly guiding himself to the first knuckle, then the second. It action drew long moans from her throat. She saw Killian share a look with his brother and a small smile. She'd had no idea so much sensation could come from having that area caressed.

Dain rubbed over her labia and slid into her pussy with two fingers. Moira's hips jumped at the feeling of having both orifices filled at one time. Pleasure ran through her body, making her tighten her grip on the blankets. Moisture coursed out of her, mixing with the oil and making their penetration of her slipperier and easier.

Killian groaned and his cock jumped in his hand. "Sweet Anot, Moira. Your body was made for this kind of play. Even now you relax and widen yourself for me."

He withdrew to drizzle more of the oil onto her anus, then slid two fingers into her. She gasped, then moaned at the sensation of him stretching her muscles so exquisitely. It hurt just a little...just enough to make pleasure pulse her clit and sear up her backbone.

"Ah, yes, Moira," murmured Dain. "You're beyond sweet and beautiful. Perfect. You can have no idea the effect this has on Killian and I," he added in a low, strained voice.

"Take me," she whispered. "I can't stand this teasing much longer."

"Soon," Killian answered. "Soon, we will." He paused. "When you are ready to take us both."

She closed her eyes and they increased the pace of their thrusts. They stroked into her in tandem, working her pussy and anus with a masterful precision that nearly made her scream. She felt the muscles of her anus ease for Killian's invasion. The pain receded and was replaced with pure ecstasy. Dain twisted his wrist, changed the angle of his thrust so that his finger rasped over that place deep within where it felt the best.

"Come for us," Dain whispered. "Moira, let it go."

Finally. Colors swirled before her eyes as their thrusts grew longer, deeper, harder. Her whole world narrowed to their possession of her body. She clenched her fists and bucked in his lap as her climax hit her. She screamed out the pleasure of it, thrusting her hips forward as if looking for a cock to fill her.

After the full force of her climax had hit her, but before her spasms had completely receded, Killian and Dain pulled away. Dain lay down flat on the bed and Killian guided her still shaking body to straddle him. Anxious and needy, she lowered her dripping pussy down on his cock and impaled herself. Dain groaned low and grasped her waist and she threw her head back and panted out her satisfaction at feeling the thick length of him filling her up.

"Moira," he murmured.

She dropped her head and kissed him, letting her hair fall around them like curtains.

"You feel so good inside me, Dain," she murmured. "So right. So perfect."

He brushed her hair away from her face in a tender gesture and caught and held her gaze. "I know," he answered softly. Something moved through his eyes. "My brother will feel as good."

Killian mounted her from behind. She felt the press and the heat of his chest against her back and the thrust of the wide crown of his cock against her nether hole. He'd coated it with a great deal of the oil, but that didn't stop her from tensing every muscle in her body. Two fingers was one thing. His long, wide cock quite another. She moved her hips, in sudden anxiety of having Killian's cock in her nether hole. How could her body accommodate two men at once?

"Hush, Moira," said Dain. "We wouldn't attempt this if you weren't ready. You will know a pleasure like never before if you allow us to proceed."

She hesitated and then nodded.

Killian reached down around her waist, into the small space between her body and Dain's, and gently stroked her clit. It responded instantly to his touch. It felt swollen and sensitive and oddly vulnerable to Killian's touch. Her hips thrust forward involuntarily and her breath hissed out of her as his oiled finger caressed her. "There, that's it, love. Just relax and open yourself to me. You can take my cock here," he purred. "Your body was made for this."

She shuddered as her pleasure centers fired to life once more. Her pussy and her anus felt needy. She ached with it. It seemed impossible that she should want more of them after the three climaxes she'd had, and yet...oh, *she did*. Suddenly, she couldn't wait to be filled by them both at once.

Killian kept petting her clit as he pushed against her anus. Dain captured a nipple in his mouth and laved over the distended peak. The slick, smooth crown of Killian's cock breached her and she cried out, clutching fistfuls of blanket on either side of Dain's head. "Oh, yes," she hissed. "It's good. Oh, sweet Goddess, so good."

Killian let out a grunt behind her and eased himself in a little farther. She felt *impaled*, deliciously, erotically so. She felt completely at their mercy with her legs spread and sandwiched between them, and yet she'd never felt safer or more cherished in her life.

"Ah, yes, love," Killian murmured. "You feel so good around my cock. You're so hot and tight and—" he groaned.

Inch by mind-blowing inch, Killian thrust himself within her until he was seated to the base. It hurt, there was no question of that, but the pleasure made the pain seem like nothing. In fact, the pain seemed to enhance the pleasure of it.

Dain pulled her down to him and laid a kiss to her lips. "Hold still," he murmured. They started to move.

Suddenly thought was barely attainable.

They moved very slowly and carefully. Dain dug his heels into the bed and thrust upward into her body, while Killian penetrated her from behind, driving deeply into the heart of her.

She moaned long and low and cried out at the top of her lungs. She'd never known pleasure could be this intense. Had never thought it was even possible. It was almost overwhelming.

Almost.

Moira climaxed hard and fast. Darkness clouded her vision for a moment as she fought to retain consciousness. Dain groaned at the violent convulsing of her pussy around his length. She felt her come lubricate her pussy, making the easy thrust of his cock into her body slicker. Still, they worked themselves in and out of her, quickening their pace. Their sounds of pleasure mixed and melded, bouncing off the walls of the chamber. Never had she felt so deliciously and utterly *possessed* as she did now.

Her last orgasm tipped her straight into another one. Her body shook and her breath came faster. They shafted into her faster and little harder and her climax extended, taking over her whole world.

The feel of their bodies sandwiching her and the slick, sweaty slide of their skin over hers was heaven. Their breathing and combined moans fired her senses. She loved the knowledge that they were completely focused on her in this moment, deriving pleasure from her body and wanting to provide her with the same.

Dain grabbed the back of her head and pulled her mouth to his. He kissed her, his tongue filling her mouth, dancing against hers. He consumed all her sounds of pleasure. He thrust up as far as he could within her and she felt his cock jump. He groaned erotically against her lips and she felt him shoot his come deep into her. Behind her, Killian gasped and also released himself.

Breathing heavily, Dain pulled her down on his body completely. Killian slid out from her and Dain rolled her over, so she lay beneath him. His breath came as hard and fast as hers and their combined come and the oil they'd used on her made her slippery between her thighs. Dain fisted his hand gently in her hair and kissed her long and hard. Then he pulled away and stared down at her with an intensity that made her heart catch and her body flare, unbelievably, to life once again beneath him.

"Ah, Moira," Dain groaned raggedly in her ear. "You are my heaven. You give me peace." He stayed that way for a long time and Moira held onto him and closed her eyes.

Eventually, Dain pulled free of her body, a loss she lamented, and pulled her close, spooning her from behind. Killian covered her other side, laying kisses to her lips before settling down and closing his eyes. A comfortable, satisfied lethargy stole over her body. She hurt all over her body, but it was a delicious soreness. One she wouldn't trade for anything.

Soon, feeling cuddled and warm and safe nestled between their large bodies, her breathing deepened to that of sleep and she drifted off.

When she awoke, the fire was again blazing, tended by someone's careful hand. Moira found herself positioned lovingly under the thick, warm blankets of the bed. She turned onto her side and saw a man's back. Her lips curving into a smile, she reached out and touched his hair. Dain. He'd stayed with her the entire night. A warm feeling spread through her chest.

Dain roused at her touch and turned over. Her face fell. Her smile dissolved.

Killian.

"You look disappointed, Moira," Killian said softly. He reached out and wrapped a tendril of her hair around his finger. "Did we not please each other well last night?"

A smile flickered over her lips. She smoothed her palm down his stubbled cheek. "Oh, yes, we did, indeed," she murmured.

"Still you are not contented to find me in your bed when you awaken?"

She hesitated a moment, then pushed the blankets away and grabbed the wrap someone—likely Dain—had laid on the end of the bed for her...before he'd left. She threw it on against the morning's chill and found a pair of slippers. She slipped those on too.

Killian sat up in the bed. The blankets fell to his waist, revealing the muscled expanse of his chest. He crossed his arms over his knees and the action defined his biceps. His handsome face wore a confused expression, making tears prick her eyes. Any other woman would take him up on his proposal in the blink of an eye. Any woman, especially one like her, poor and without prospects, would be lucky and honored to even be noticed by such a man as Killian.

And yet.

And yet, she wanted the damaged brother. She wanted the brother who was destined to break her heart and shred her soul. It made no since that it should be Dain and not Killian who fired her blood and made her heart beat faster. It made no sense that it should be Dain she loved and not Killian.

Ah, what was wrong with her? Her common sense and her brain said she should prefer Killian...but her heart wanted only one man, Dain.

"Moira?" Killian asked. "What is it?"

She gathered her long hair up and knotted it at the nape of her neck. As she did, she flashed him a half-smile. "Nothing is wrong, Killian."

He pushed out of the bed and padded over to her naked. When he reached her, he placed his hands on her shoulders and made her look at him. "You are lying. I can see it in your eyes. May I take a guess at why you're upset?"

She looked up at him with her lips parted.

"You love my brother," he said in a tender voice. "I knew that before, Moira. I told you that before, remember? There's no need to feel guilt that you don't feel the same way about me as you do for him. Last night, the way you looked at each of us and the way you touched." He shook his head. "There is no doubt in my mind that he loves you."

She tried to turn her head, but he caught her chin. She looked up at him with a tremble in her lower lip and tears sheened her eyes.

"When you turned over this morning...you thought it was Dain who had stayed, not me," he said softly.

She hesitated and then nodded.

Killian crushed her to him and kissed the crown of her head. He let out a little laugh. "Moira, don't you understand? I'm happy that you love him and not me. Dain needs your love more than I do." He ran his fingers through her hair and she wound her arms around his waist, breathing in the masculine scent of him. "As I said before, I want to help you reach him. I want to help you breach his defenses. I think my brother wanted me here last night in part to form a barrier between you and him. Perhaps you're getting to him, Moira, but he doesn't know how to react to it. Maybe it frightens. If I can help him be close to you, I will do that." He shook his head. "And don't give another thought to guilt, please?"

"I'm sorry," she murmured. She shifted so she could stare up into his face. "You must already know I can't marry you. Not even if Dain pushes me away in the end. I could never marry you."

He bent his head and kissed her tenderly on the lips. "I like you and I respect you. We would've made a good match, but I never loved you, Moira. Not in the way you love Dain. It's all right if you don't entertain my request."

Moira let out a breath she hadn't even known she'd been keeping. She pulled away and Killian let her. He went for his clothes and started putting them on.

"But…Dain…" she whispered barely loud enough for him to hear. "He will never be ready for the feelings I have to bestow. It's a lost cause."

Killian pulled his shirt over his head and paused, sighing. "Honestly, Moira, my brother is largely a mystery to me. I don't pretend to understand his heart. I know I saw him touch you, look at you, last night with a love I've never seen before within him. But whether or not he's ready to acknowledge those feelings. Well, that I do not know."

"I know," she answered softly. She walked toward the door, but paused before she left the room. "You are an amazing man, Killian. One day you will find a woman you will love at first sight. It will be strong and passionate and undeniable. She will love you back at first sight. I vow it."

He gave her a half-smile. "Is that a prophecy?" he asked in a teasing voice.

She returned his gaze in all seriousness. "I feel it deeply within me, Killian. It is a knowingness that this event lies strong and deep in your future." She left the room and traveled back to her own chamber. It was indeed in his future. She could feel it in every part of her body.

But she also felt her own future…and that one was not as bright. It was filled with agonizing pain and darkness. Perhaps death.

Chapter Seven

ॐ

Moira led her mare out of the stable and checked the saddle's cinching and made sure her supply bags were well secured. Blix and Athna lay near her, looking up at her with their dark, soulful eyes. They sensed she was leaving.

It had grown so warm over the last couple of weeks that she could keep her mittens off while she worked outside. The sun had just risen and gray still colored the sky. Clouds did not however, she would have plenty of light to travel by come the evening.

It was time to go to the Port of Paradise. The snow had melted enough to ensure her safe passage and the cold lessened every passing day.

She gave Blix and Athna one more good tummy rub and kissed their sleek heads in farewell. Moira pulled her hood over her head, donned her heavy woolen mittens and mounted the mare. When the horse, unaccustomed to bearing a rider because it had been stabled for so long a time, danced beneath her, she looked back at the castle a final time.

She'd chosen the dawn to leave in order to avoid any sorrowful goodbyes. She didn't want to tell William, Bess, Killian…or Dain goodbye.

Especially Dain.

Biting back a sudden choke of tears in her throat, she turned the mare's head toward the gateway of Aeodan and began her journey.

In the three weeks since her encounter with Killian and Dain, she and Dain had made love several more times. She went to him sometimes in the dead of night and he rolled her beneath his body and took her slowly, so slowly and carefully and with so much love in his gaze that her climax shattered her and left her in tears.

Every time, when she awoke the next morning, it was to an empty bed.

At times, he would come to her chamber and they would rip each other's clothes off and worship each other's bodies over and over until dawn. When she awoke, the fire was tended and she was comfortable and warm in her bed…and he was gone. The encounters left her wondering if she'd simply dreamed them.

She touched her stomach. She hoped she'd gained a child from him. Oh, how she did. He'd asked her repeatedly if she wanted him to use precautions against it. There was an herbal brew she could take to prevent pregnancy, or he could pull out of her before he came. Always, she said no.

She crested the large hill opposite the castle and spotted the road that would lead her to the Port of Paradise. She turned and looked back at the castle one last time, then turned the mare and started down the path.

At noon, she heard the pounding of hooves on the road behind her. Fearing brigands, she quickly led the mare into the tree line and drew the short sword attached to the saddle sheath and held it at the ready. She hadn't lived for so long alone in the woods that she hadn't learned how to protect herself.

Two hooded figures, one on a monstrously huge black horse and the other on a white of an equal size came into her view as she peered between the branches of the trees. She prayed her mare would stay quiet, but she stepped to the side and broke a branch.

The riders stopped. Her heart lodged itself somewhere just south of her tonsils.

"Moira?" called one.

Killian.

She sheathed her sword and stepped out of the tree line. "Killian? Dain?"

They urged their horses toward her.

"Why did you follow me?" she asked.

Dain's black mount stepped forward. "Why did you leave like a thief before dawn?" His voice held an edge of steel. His eyes were angry.

"I-I thought it would be easier that way."

Dain's mount drew up next to her. Her mare tossed her head at the close proximity of the other horse. "We will not allow you to travel to the Port of Paradise alone, Moira."

She set her mouth into a thin, hard line. "This is my business, not yours. I have no wish to involve you." She flashed a look at Killian. "Either of you."

Dain reached out and gently caught her chin. He guided her gaze to his. His light blue eyes swirled with anger. "You involved me the moment I saw you at my front gate, the moment you allowed me to bed you, my lady. This *does* concern me." He released her and backed his mount up a few paces. "It concerns both of us."

"What if you have an attack between here and the Port of Paradise, Moria?" asked Killian with a frown.

She shrugged. "I would deal with it as I dealt with the attacks before I met you. I'm well accustomed to taking care of myself."

"Perhaps it's time you became accustomed to someone taking care of you," said Dain. Before she could respond, he turned his mount toward the Port of Paradise. "Let's go," he said gruffly.

She and Killian watched Dain ride ahead, then Killian drew his stallion by her mare for the journey. Dain stayed ahead for most of the day, drawing close only to discuss with them something pertaining to the logistics of their travel.

"He seems very agitated," Moira commented as she stared at Dain's rigid back. "I hope it's not because of me."

"I think he wonders if we will truly find Cyric is all, Moira. I believe that is what troubles him."

The sun had begun to dip below the mountains to their west, but the sky remained bright and cloudless. Perhaps they would travel for a ways longer before they stopped. The road to the Port of Paradise leading from the territory of Aeoli was not for the faint of heart. It would take them two days of hard riding to reach their destination, the capitol city of New Ecasia.

"Tell me, Killian. I never asked before. I know your brother has the wings of a white owl, but what wings do you possess? Do you have the same since you're twins?"

He shook his head and smiled. "I inherited the same wings of Rue d'Ange, our famous ancestor. I have the wings of a falcon. Would you like to see?" He unfurled them slowly, so as to not spook the horses. They stretched broad and long and beautiful with a multitude of gray and black shading.

"They're gorgeous," she breathed. She reached out and ran her fingers down the soft wingtip of one. "Truly."

"Trying to impress Moira with your wingspan, Killian?" Dain called out from ahead.

"And why not?" Killian shouted back with a laugh. Slowly, he folded them back into his body.

Three hours later they came to a small cabin set back in the woods. "It's a hunting lodge," explained Killian as he pushed the door open. "We use it to stop over whenever we travel to the Port of Paradise."

The interior was furnished with what appeared to be handmade furniture. There was one large bed in the center of the room and several pallets and smaller mattresses scattered around the edge of the room. A long table stood in one corner near one of the fireplaces. Another fireplace stood at the opposite end of the cabin. Dain and Killian began the job of gathering wood to make fires to heat the cold building and Moira located some sheets and blankets and made up the largest of the beds.

The temperature had dropped when the sun had gone down and Moira figured that because of the night they'd all shared together, they wouldn't think her forward if she suggested they all sleep together to conserve warmth. Perhaps even Dain might swallow his revulsion and sleep by her side for the entire night. She threw the pillows to the head of the bed a little more forcefully than she'd intended at the thought. A tendril of her hair came loose from its coiffure and she blew it angrily out of her eyes.

"All right?" asked Dain, coming in with an armful of wood.

"Fine," she said softly as she hooked the tendril behind her ear. She watched him with hungry eyes as he dropped the load near the hearth and started to break the kindling. She wanted him so much it made her chest hurt. "I'll get the flatbread I've got in my saddlebags," she said and went for the door.

Dain stood and caught her arm as she passed. She looked down at it and then up into his eyes, her lips parted. Dear sweet Goddess! His slightest touch made her needy.

"Killian caught a wild hare and is preparing it for the spit."

"The bread can accompany — "

He pulled her toward him and kissed her, cutting off the rest of her sentence. "Moira," he breathed. He set his forehead against hers. "You frightened me this morning. I was afraid when I felt you'd left the castle on your own."

Her eyes widened. "You felt?"

He nodded. "Perhaps it's..."

"A bit of your magick."

"Or maybe it's a connection you and I share. We do share one, you and I, but you must know that, that—"

She leaned up and kissed him. Tears choked her eyes and throat. "I know," she whispered brokenly. Grief welled up inside her. "Please don't say it out loud." Then she whirled and left the cabin.

She practically ran to her mare. Hurriedly, she fought to get the saddlebag open and sought within for the flatbread. She freed it and stood looking down at the small leather-bound package. Then tears clouded her vision and she leaned against the horse, letting a couple of them fall. They splashed into the leather and she watched with clouded vision as they rolled off to the ground.

Behind her, she heard the cabin door open and close. Then it whined open once more. "Moira?" Killian asked. "Are you all right?"

Quickly, she wiped her eyes on the backs of the sleeves of her coat. "I'm fine." She offered a smile. "Just a bit tired, I guess."

She heard his footfalls on the ground and soon felt his body heat beside her. He reached out, turned her and pulled her up against him. Moira closed her eyes as the urge to really sob came over her. She tried her best to choke back her sadness and felt tears burn her eyes. She grasped the leather-bound package in one hand and balled her other fist against the front of Killian's heavy coat so tightly her nails bit into her palm.

Killian wrapped his arms around her and kissed the crown of her head. "You don't seem fine to me," he murmured.

She let out a small, strangled-sounding laugh. Unable to speak for a moment, too afraid her body would betray her and send her into a sobbing fit, she simply relaxed into Killian's strong, warm body, absorbing the comfort he offered her.

How badly it hurt to want something so much and be denied it. Never had she wanted the love of another more than she wanted Dain's love. It felt like a part of her soul was withering away into nothingness to see that resigned look in his eyes, to hear from his own lips that he could never love her back.

She swallowed hard and cleared her throat, having finally mastered her emotion. "I-I'll be fine." She pulled away from him a little, discreetly wiping her tears away with the back of her hand. "It's true that right now I don't feel that way, but I will be fine...eventually."

Killian looked down at her doubtfully, then bent his head and took her mouth in a long, sensual kiss. Their lips and tongues meshed and mated and Moira could taste the salt of her tears.

When her knees felt weak and pleasure thrummed up her spine, he released her. He stepped toward the cabin and motioned to her with one hand. The expression in his eyes told her that he didn't believe her. "Come. The night is cloudless and the temperature is dropping rapidly. It's getting far too cold to stay outside. We've both fires going within and the rabbit I caught is roasting."

"What of the horses?"

"There's an outbuilding a small distance away, a small stable. I'm going to take them there now and bed them down for the night."

She walked into the cabin. The small area was already growing warm. She went about the business of dusting off the table and locating the plates and utensils while Dain and Killian cared for the horses.

After they'd eaten, Dain retired to the bed and she and Killian sat up a while longer, talking in low voices near the fire. Finally, she also retired and slid under the blankets near Dain. For a moment she allowed herself the fantasy that this was their cabin, where they lived together in love, that this was just one night like any other—the routine of a mated couple.

Dain turned toward her and wrapped her in his embrace. He inhaled the scent of her hair and found the edge of her nightdress, smoothing his palms up her body as though he simply had to touch her skin.

She felt Killian slide in at her back. Together, wordlessly, he and Dain pulled the gown over her head. She ended up sandwiched between the two of them nude. Her breath started to come faster.

In silence, their hands massaged her body, rubbing over her back, her breasts, and her buttocks. Her hands roamed, too, bumping into theirs. She ran her fingers over their chests and unbuttoned their shirts and trews.

"But," she gasped as Killian sucked her nipple into his mouth. "We need our rest," she finished in a rush.

Dain pulled her beneath him and growled, "Damn the rest, we want you."

Dain kissed her, and then descended to take one of her nipples into his mouth. Killian took the other and suddenly she forgot what she'd been protesting. Moaning, she threaded her fingers through their hair as they feasted on her breasts. Their hands met at her pussy, where they worked together to push her higher and higher, sailing her into ecstasy and making her soak their hands and the sheets in her excitement.

"Taste," she murmured incoherently. "I want to taste both of you...at the same time." Goddess, she felt almost drunk on the two of them.

She pushed up and watched while they fully undressed their gorgeous bodies. They stood at the edge of the bed side-by-side, both their cocks delectably hard. She knelt at the edge and took their balls in her hands. With a noise that was almost like a purr in the back of her throat, she leaned forward and licked the crown of each of their cocks.

They both groaned and Moira closed her eyes, savoring their sounds of excitement and the fact she had both of them at the same time. She engulfed the head of Dain's cock and laved over it and she stroked up and down the length of Killian's. Over and over, she traded off, sucking and licking the shaft of one while she fondled the other. Their groans echoed through the cabin, increasing her own excitement.

They grasped her hair, rubbed her back, fondled her breasts and, when they could, dipped their hands down over her buttocks to her pussy. She was so aroused, her sex felt like a plump, reddened piece of ripe fruit.

Finally Dain broke away and mounted her from behind with a growl of anticipation. She thrust Killian's cock down her throat, taking him nearly to the base as Dain grabbed her hips and eased into her from behind.

Killian rubbed her shoulders and tangled his fingers through her loose hair as she suckled him wildly, in tempo with the state of her own arousal.

Dain let out a low groan as he seated himself balls-deep within her. He grasped her hip with one hand and leisurely began stroking her extended and needy clit with the other as he started thrusting.

Moira moaned on an outward mouth stroke. Her eyes nearly rolled to the back of her head at the delicious feeling of Dain's cock inside her and the perfect, gentle and steady way he stroked her clit nearly drove her insane.

She pulled on Killian's cock, teasing him with her tongue until his hands tightened in her hair and his hips thrust forward. Slowly, he stroked himself into her mouth. She felt his cock jump against her tongue and his body tensed. Swallowing him down, she fought to keep the back of her throat open to accept his length, while Dain eased in and out of her with powerful, steady strokes.

Moira stayed still, reveling in the way both men thrust into her body. Their groans and the sound of their breathing filled the quiet air of the cabin. Her body thrummed and pulsed with the presence of them both and the possession they exerted over her.

Finally, Killian cried out and shot down the back of her throat. She swallowed his musky come instinctively, feeling the heat of it coat her throat.

Killian pulled his cock from her and backed away. He was breathing heavily and had a dazed, satisfied look in his eyes.

Behind her, Dain picked up the pace of his thrusts, making her moan and call his name. In an instant, she found herself flat on her back. Dain mounted her and rammed himself back inside her, a possessive motion that made her gasp and arch her back.

He stared down at her with the same consumed look on his face that he always had when he made love to her. The one that made her heart rate heighten and her breath catch in her throat. He thrust relentlessly into her body with a deep, long and even pace, raising her hips up to meet his strokes. The sound of their coupling was a skin-on-skin slap.

Beside her Killian reached between their bodies and stroked her clit over and over. His intent gaze was also on her face. He used the cream that coated her pussy to lubricate her clit. The steady caress of the pad of his finger over the sensitive bundle of nerves was more than she could bear.

Moira's world shattered. Pleasure exploded out from her sex, enveloping her in complete ecstasy. She threw her head back into the pillows and screamed it out to the cabin. Above her, Dain did the same.

Spent and more than satisfied, the three of them collapsed on the bed.

Killian laughed. "Anot, woman," he growled in a rasping voice.

She let out a small laugh. "You'd think we couldn't sleep in the same bed without doing this."

Dain pulled her toward him and kissed her temple. "You're irresistible to us, Moira. You should have realized that by now."

Killian pulled her near him and laid a gentle kiss to her lips. With both men flanking her, warm from the fire and even warmer from their lovemaking, she fell asleep.

When she awoke that morning, Killian lay beside her on the bed but, even though they'd fallen asleep with their limbs entangled, Dain was gone.

Suddenly irritated beyond all reason, she threw the blankets aside, quickly donned a gown, her shoes and a cloak and went outside to find him.

He stood not far from the cabin, looking down at a frozen stream. Her breath showed in the cold morning air as she whipped him around to face her. "Why?" she demanded to know.

"Why what?"

"Why do you never allow me the pleasure of waking up beside you?"

He scooped her up in his arms and bore her backward to the trunk of a large tree. She gasped in surprise and he bent his head and kissed her soundly, even as he undid his trews. He guided her hand to his cock. It was hard. Instantly, even though she was sore from their lovemaking only hours earlier, she felt herself moisten between her thighs.

He broke the kiss. "Every time I see you, I want you, Moira. I want you. It never stops. My hunger for you is insatiable."

She stroked his cock and he groaned. "That was not an answer," she said with a lift of her brow.

And still, he didn't answer her. Instead he reached into her cloak and gathered her skirts to her waist. She didn't even feel the cold. He found her bare pussy and stroked and teased and impaled her with his long and masterful fingers until her cream ran down her inner thighs and she'd forgotten her question. Dain could make her aroused with a look. His touch was enough to make her forget how to breathe, how to think. He was like some fine, sweet alcohol she'd become addicted to. She didn't know how she'd be able to give him up. In this moment she simply wanted to pretend like she would never have to.

He cupped her buttocks and lifted her. He slid her easily down on his erection and held her pinned between his body and the tree. They were eye to eye, connected by both gaze and sex. It was more intimate than anything she'd ever experienced.

"If I could, I'd spend the rest of my life buried inside you." He kissed her tenderly and started to thrust. "The one place I can find peace is within your arms."

She kissed him back, twining her fingers through the hair at his nape and let him take her up against the tree. He stroked into her until her pussy spasmed and convulsed in pleasure around his shaft, until he groaned low in her ear and lost himself inside her. When it was over, he held onto her tightly, whispering her name over and over in her ear.

She closed her eyes and hoped fervently for his child.

Something, anything, that she could keep of him.

Chapter Eight

ဆာ

The Port of Paradise rose like a city made by the Goddess' hand as they approached it from the north. Dain felt awed by it every time he came here.

Towers and tall buildings of every color stone imaginable rose from behind the thick city walls. The Port of Paradise had sustained some damage during the war, but the citizens had repaired most of it so the scars were barely visible.

The city stood on an inlet to the great ocean that surrounded New Ecasia on three sides. It was a small territory unto itself on the border of Sudhra Territory and Nordan Territory. Lord Gregor and his wife, the Lady Anaisse, had founded the city, believing that in order to heal the rift between the countries after the Sudhraian–Nordanese war that it was important for the governing lords and ladies to do so from a neutral place.

"Oh, dear Goddess," exclaimed Moira to his left.

"Have you ever been here?" he asked her.

She shook her head, her eyes wide. "I never imagined it would be so immense!"

They entered by the north gates. The guards gave them little notice as they passed but to salute both himself and Killian. The emblems they wore on their cloaks marked them as having been officers in the New Ecasian military during the war. That awarded them a measure of respect.

They led their horses through the gates and into seeming chaos. The din of the city met their ears first—street hawkers crying out in an effort to sell their fresh fish, meat pies, hair ribbons and other trinkets. The sounds of horses' hooves and carriage wheels on the cobblestones and the sound of chatter and laughter completed the cacophony.

The scent of the ocean nearby tinted the air with a briny smell. It mixed with the scent of the city, horse dung, humanity, and the grease from cook fires. It was a pungent odor that marked the city distinctly as the Port of Paradise.

Moira stopped her horse in the center of it all and openly gaped.

Killian tugged on her reins and laughed. "Come on, little love. We should find lodging before nightfall."

They traveled down the main road, past the cook shops, the dressmakers, the blacksmiths and the pubs. Finally, they found an inn that didn't seem too grungy and that advertised hot water and hot food.

The stable boy took their mounts and for an extra half-crown that Killian flipped to him said he'd bring their bags in for them.

The interior of the establishment was mostly clean. A large fire roared in one corner and tables lined the large downstairs eating area. The acrid smell of candle wax, cooking food and travelers' unwashed bodies assaulted their noses as soon as they entered.

The innkeeper, a burly middle-aged man with bright red hair, told them there were two rooms left in the inn. They took them both and ordered baths for the three of them, plus hot meals, sent to their rooms.

They were only too happy to escape up the stairs, room keys in hand.

Moira went to the first room and unlocked her door. She supposed that now they were in town, it was back to reality. Dain would likely stay with his brother. The door opened and she cast one, hopefully not too pathetically forlorn, look at the two men.

"What in the Underworld are you doing, Dain?" said Killian as he elbowed him aside and stepped through the doorway of the room next to hers. He winked at her right before he said, "This room is mine alone. Find another one to stay in," and shut the door in Dain's face.

Dain stilled for a moment in front of the door. The lock slammed home on the other side. She couldn't see the expression on Dain's face because of the shadows. Hand still on the doorknob, key in one hand, she watched him.

After a heartbeat, he turned and walked toward her. "I hope you don't mind."

She shook her head and pushed the door open. Strange comment considering all they'd done together over the last few months, but the city did seem to throw reality into sharp relief. Being here made all the rest seem somewhat like a dream…a bittersweet dream for her.

They walked into the simply decorated room. A bed barely large enough for two people stood along one wall. A dresser stood along the opposite wall, and a large brass bathtub dominated a corner. There was one window that had a view out onto the main thoroughfare.

The boy delivered their bags and a serving girl brought up a hot meal of roast beef with vegetables and two tankards of ale.

"So, we're here," said Dain after he'd swallowed a mouthful. "What now?"

She took a careful sip of her ale. "I don't know yet. I felt strongly that I was to come here. Now I have to…trust that we will be led to him." She shrugged. "Or he to us. After that, I'm not sure."

Dain fell silent. He kept eating.

"If we find him, Dain, how will you feel? What will you do?"

He set his forkful of food down on his plate and got up. He paced to the window and leaned against the frame, staring down at the crush of people. "I don't know," he said softly.

He felt her soft grasp on his arm. "Will you...kill him for what he did with Andreea? For betraying your friendship and your trust while you were away at war?"

"No!" he said forcefully. When she backed away from him, he softened his voice. "No. Andreea had as much a part to play as Cyric did in what happened." He closed his eyes and rubbed his hand over his stubbled chin. "There's been far too much killing already. I don't want any more blood on my hands. I say I'd kill him, but..." He shook his head. "I'm tired of death."

She stroked the back of her hand across his cheek. "That's what makes you a real man, Dain. That's why I...care so much for you."

He caught her hand and turned her toward him. "But never mistake me for a good man, Moira. All right? Never do that. It may mean your life."

Her eyes widened, but he pushed past her. Someone knocked on the door. It was the serving boys bringing in the first batch of hot water for their baths. Moira could have her bath first. After she'd finished, they'd pull the plug in the bottom of the tub and drain the water out, then fill it again for him.

They waited until the serving boys were finished, then Dain pulled Moira toward him and kissed her tenderly. This woman gave him peace. She was the only person who'd ever been able to do that. With love in his every gesture, he undressed her and lowered her into the bathtub. Using the lavender-scented chunk of soap they'd left, he devotedly washed her hair and every square inch of her body. As though he loved her, worshiped her, adored her. He felt all these things and more.

He wished he could keep her.

After they'd both bathed and he'd made love to her until her cries had shaken the walls of the room, he pulled her close under the blankets of the bed and ran his fingers through her hair. He enjoyed so much the feel of her bare body against his.

"Tomorrow we should go to the Tower of Governance and request an audience. Descendants of the Firsts always get priority. They may know the whereabouts of Cyric," he murmured before they fell asleep.

* * * * *

The morning dawned with the sweet promise of spring in the air. The birds in the trees that dotted the cobblestone street warbled their satisfaction to the world at large.

Moira threw open the window in the room and breathed in the scent of the city. It was warm, so much warmer than it had been in the mountains of Aeoli. Only one thing dampened her spirits.

When she'd awoken, Dain had once again been gone.

She turned from the window and returned to sit on the edge of the bed. She supposed she should be accustomed to it by now, but every time she woke up alone, she felt sadness.

A knock sounded on the door and she got up to answer it. Dain and Killian both stood on the other side with boxes in their hands. They each wore new clothing. Each of them greeted her with kisses and set the boxes down on the bed. She followed after them, curious.

Dain wore all black. Black knee-high leather riding boots sheathed his feet. Tucked into the tops of the boots was a pair of well-made, expensive-looking soft doeskin trews. He wore a finely woven black shirt with ties at the top. The leather ties were undone, revealing a mouthwatering peek at his smoothly muscled chest. He'd even bound his hair at his neck with a black leather thong.

Killian's clothing was almost identical to his brother's, save his boots were brown and his shirt white.

"I awoke this morning and could sleep no more, so Killian and I went out to buy clothes fit for a visit to the Tower of Governance," said Dain. He flipped the top of one box and pulled out an exquisitely made dark green gown. "I took the liberty of selecting one for you. I thought this color would go best with your hair, eyes and skin tone."

Moira put a hand to her lips to stop herself from reaching out and touching it. She'd never had anything so finely made or expensive. She'd never worn such material close to her skin.

Killian pulled a light green over-corset that dangled with small sun and moon charms, a white linen underdress from another box and then a pair of white slippers.

"It's lovely," she finally breathed.

Dain laid it on the bed. "I cannot wait to see you in it, Moira. We will send a woman to help you dress. With that corset, you'll need it."

They left the room and Moira reached out and touched the gown, rubbing the soft material between her thumb and forefinger.

Someone knocked on the door and she jumped, startled. The maid called through the door, then entered.

An hour later had Moira outfitted in the decadent clothing and her hair in a twist on the back of her head. The maid had pulled a few loose tendrils down around her face and at the back of her neck and curled them to soften the look.

Moira thanked the maid for her help and went downstairs to meet Dain and Killian.

They stood outside laughing and talking with the stable boy. These were two men who didn't believe in class difference. She loved them both for that.

Killian glanced at her and did a double take. He pressed a hand to his heart and fell back against the outside wall of the inn in exaggeration. "Moira, you look stunning. Do we have to leave now, or can we go up to the room for a little while?" He grinned mischievously.

Dain just stared at her with a small smile on his lips and a heated look in his eyes. He didn't have to say anything at all. How he thought she looked was in his gaze and it made her blush deeply and look away.

The stable boy brought their horses and they made their way through the Port of Paradise toward the ocean and the Tower of Governance.

Moira inhaled sharply when they reached the eastern part of the city and the Alban Ocean came into view. On her left and right bustled the city in all its noisy and fragrant beauty. Straight ahead of her, past the end of the road, past a sandy beach, lay the blue-green tranquil waters of the sea. She'd never seen such a large body of water before. Her fingers curled tighter on the reins of her mount. "It's so beautiful," she murmured.

Dain looked over at her. "Perhaps, when this over and your attacks are cured, we can go there."

She offered him a tight smile. The words were nice, the sentiment pretty, but doubt and fear shone clearly in his eyes and it chilled her heart rather than warmed it. When this was over, she would return home to her cottage in the woods, and Dain would go back to being a hermit in his castle.

And her heart would be shredded beyond all hope of repair.

A few moments later, Killian and Dain led her to the left, down a street filled with expensive bakeshops, chocolatiers and fine dressmakers. In front of her rose a tall white tower with a golden dome.

"Is that the Tower of Governance?" she asked.

Killian turned toward her. "The one and only. That's where the Council of Ministers and the Grand Lord Elect dispute—er, *discuss*—state matters of governance for the three territories."

"Who there will help us?" Before she'd known Dain and Killian were coming with her, she'd thought of coming to the Tower of Governance for help. Now that she saw the imposing structure and the highly guarded entrance, she was thankful they'd come along.

"The magicked sons and daughters of the First Borns are always welcome there and Dain and I know several of the ministers personally." Killian cleared his throat. "Everyone will be shocked by Dain's appearance in the city."

Moira hadn't even thought of that. Having spent so much time with Dain, she'd forgotten what the rest of the world believed about him, what she'd believed about him so long ago. No doubt those who knew who he was would look askance at him, perhaps fear him.

They reached the gates and Killian murmured a few words to the four guards who policed the entrance to the tower. All of them glanced at Dain before allowing them admittance.

They passed through the gates and into a large manicured lawn, though which led a flower-lined cobblestone road. At the end, in a large circular drive, rose a fountain with a statue of Lord Gregor and Lady Anaisse, the founders of the Port of Paradise and the architects of the current system of governance.

Stable hands ran out and took their horses and she, Killian and Dain entered through the tall, carved wooden doors that led into the marble and glass foyer of the tower. A man dressed in a silk green and gold tunic rose from where he sat behind a large glass table and approached them.

"Good afternoon, my lords." He inclined his head toward Moira. "My lady. How may I be of service?"

Dain stepped forward. "I am Dain d'Ange." The man's eyes widened at his name. His body went noticeably stiff. Dain continued as though everything were completely normal, as though one of the most mysterious and dangerous men of New Ecasia hadn't just walked into the Tower of Governance. Dain turned toward her and Killian. "This is my brother, Killian d'Ange and that is Moira ki Sienne, named for her direct ancestor. We've come in hopes of obtaining a private audience with Minister Barrow or Minister Christo."

The man lifted a gray eyebrow. "In regards to…?"

"Well, that is private. Barrow and Christo are both personal friends of our father. I'm sure either of them would be willing to take five minutes out of their schedule to have a word with us."

The man hesitated, raking his gaze up and down Dain and grimacing slightly. Finally, he turned. "I'll see what I can do," he said as he left the foyer.

Dain turned back to them, brows raised. "I see that my reputation precedes me."

They stood in the entryway for a long while, watching people come and go. Moira had a mind to tell the stuffy foyer monitor to order some chairs installed. Finally, the double doors at the opposite end of the foyer opened and a tall woman walked through. She was tall and thin, with salt-and-pepper hair secured in a bun. The long white robes of a Minister of Governance adorned her.

A big smile lit up her fine-boned face. "Killian, Dain! It's been a long time," the woman said as she approached them with an outstretched hand.

Dain shook her hand and the woman pulled him into an embrace. "Minister Christo," Dain greeted.

"Minister?" the woman exclaimed with a light laugh. "Never minister to you two. Dain, it is so good to see you away from that castle." She turned to Killian and greeted him with the same enthusiasm.

"Christo, this is Moira, she is a magicked direct descendant of the Lady Sienne," Killian introduced.

Christo took her hand and squeezed it warmly. Moira instantly liked her.

"I'm delighted to meet you," said Christo. "Now, let's go into my chambers. I have only a few minutes to spare between my meetings. The minister's work is never done, I'm afraid."

They followed Christo through the double doors into a huge round room where ministers and their secretaries were engaged in conversation, sometimes very heated discussions, with other men and women who were dressed in expensive formal tunics and gowns.

Christo turned toward her, marking their inquisitive stares. "Ministers take the counsel of their regional representatives on a variety of issues between the governance meetings," she explained. The din filled the large room, making it difficult for Moira to hear Christo.

Christo led them around the edge of the round room and out one of the many doors Moira could see. As soon as they closed the heavy carved wooden door behind them, the sound completely stopped. All was silent.

Their footsteps echoed down the hallway as Christo led them past more wooden doors and small tables set with vases of fresh flowers. Finally, they came to a door carved with the image of a large winged man.

"You're an Aeolian minister," exclaimed Moira.

Christo opened the door and ushered them within her office. "One of five allotted to the territory."

They entered the wood-paneled office and Christo turned. "So, I brought you here because undoubtedly what you've come to request of me is private. It must be important to have drawn Dain to the Port of Paradise." She sat on the edge of a large marble-topped desk. "What is it you require?"

"We'd hoped you'd know the whereabouts of Lord Cyric H'valric," stated Dain without preamble.

Christo stiffened visibly. "Well, of all the things you could've asked me, I never figured on that." She paused and pursed her lips together. "Why do you ask, Dain?"

"He doesn't ask for himself, Minister Christo. He asks on my behalf," Moira broke in. "I'm the one who desires to find Cyric, not Killian or Dain."

Christo turned her blue eyes in Moira's direction. "And why?"

"I am magicked, blessed with a small amount of precognitive ability. Sometimes I can see or feel what lies in the future, and sometimes I have visions. For a while now, I have been having visions of Lord Cyric and Lord Dain. They're accompanied with painful headaches and sometimes cause me to lose consciousness. When I sought out Dain, I ceased having attacks that featured him." She paused.

"But you still have them of Cyric and feel the need to seek him out for some reason," Christo finished for her.

"Yes."

Christo turned her gaze back to Dain. "The problem is that Dain may want to kill Cyric."

Moira watched a muscle work in Dain's jaw. His spine went rigid. It was apparent how much this entire trip was costing him.

"I thought you didn't believe Dain capable of murder," said Killian softly. "I thought you never believed Dain killed Andreea."

"I don't," Christo answered.

"Then what's the problem?" asked Killian.

Christo rose from her perch on the edge of the desk and walked to a wall with various framed documents. "I don't believe Dain killed Andreea. He loved her. I've known Dain since he was a child and he doesn't have such a crime within his heart. There is no question of that. Not even if the war had disturbed him. Not even if he does indeed hold dark magick within himself." She speared Dain with a hard gaze. "No matter what Dain may say to the contrary. There is some other explanation for what happened. As you'll remember, I fought for Dain's release after the incident on the grounds of a lack of evidence."

"I remember well, Christo," said Killian. "I and my family thank you for that."

Christo turned toward him. "However Dain doesn't love Cyric, it is safe to say. One may go so far as to say Cyric is responsible for all the woe in Dain's life. Therefore, there is a chance that Dain may take revenge on him."

"I don't want to be in the same room with Cyric, Christo," said Dain in a low voice. "I don't even want to breathe the same air as Cyric. I am doing this for Moira. It's as simple as that. I have no intention of even touching him—" He bit the end of the sentence off as if suddenly realizing that with his particular brand of magick he wouldn't need to touch him.

145

Christo turned toward Moira with a small smile on her lips and a speculative look in her eyes. "Well, well," she murmured almost to herself. Then louder, "Fine. So be it. I do know where Cyric is. Dain, please leave the room."

"Why?" asked Killian.

Christo shrugged. "If you choose to share the information I'm about to give with Dain afterward, I have no control over that. I simply don't want to be the one responsible for giving it to him."

"I'll leave," said Dain. He turned and left the room.

Christo waited until Dain had closed the door behind him before she spoke. "You'll find Cyric in Sarar City, Sudhra. It lies in the most southern tip of the territory. It's far, about an eight-day's journey from the Port of Paradise. It is not a large city. You will not have trouble finding him once you arrive." She raised her hands. "I do not recommend telling this to Dain, and I highly discourage you from taking him with you."

Killian snorted. "As though we could stop him." He glanced at Moira. "She needs to find him and there's no possible way Dain will allow her to do it on her own."

Christo gave her a slow smile. "Yes, I understand that he cares for her. It's quite apparent in the way he looks at her. This is very good."

Moira gave her head a shake. "You're mistaken."

Christo laughed. "Hardly."

The door opened and a young man stuck his head within the room. "Minister Christo, the agricultural meeting is beginning."

Christo nodded and the man retreated. "I must leave you now. Good luck."

"Thank you, Minister Christo," said Moira from her heart.

"Thank you," said Killian.

"My pleasure...and slight apprehension." She moved to the door. "Don't be a stranger, Killian, and give my regards to Dain."

They followed her out the door and watched her retreat. Dain joined them moments after Christo had disappeared back through the door at the end of the corridor.

"Where are we going?" Dain asked in a flat voice.

Killian and Moira exchanged a glance. "Sudhra," said Killian.

Once back at the hotel, they ordered food brought up and ate in Dain and Moira's room. Everyone seemed at once relieved that they finally knew where to find Cyric, and somewhat on edge as well.

Dain ate silently, with an intense expression on his face that seemed mostly focused on her.

She took a sip of wine and watched as he watched her lips on the rim of her glass and her throat swallow. Goddess, just his hot, predatory gaze could make her sex cream.

"Are you all right?" she asked, looking downward.

He stood without a word and took her hand, pulling her to her feet. Killian caught her gaze as Dain pulled her to him and crushed her mouth to his. She closed her eyes under the onslaught of his mouth and felt Killian at her back, his hands running over her body.

She closed her eyes and tipped her back, enjoying the feeling of four possessive male hands on her body. Dain bent his head and gently bit the tender place where her throat joins her shoulder, sending shivers through her already powerfully aroused body. She traced her hands down the front of his chest, feeling the bunch of his muscles, and found his cock through his trews. He was hard for her.

The only sound was their breathing and the rustle of her clothing coming off. She stood naked between them, her breasts full and her nipples excited. She pulled at Killian's shirt, but he stopped her. Together, he and Dain moved her to the bed and laid her down. Each of them came down on opposite sides of her, their hands exploring her.

She tried to roll toward Dain, but he stopped her. He pressed both her hands above her head on the mattress and stared into her eyes. "You are bound and unable to move, Moira. You can't see the ropes or feel them, but they're there."

She bit her lip and nodded. Killian dragged his fingers up her hot, swollen sex and her eyes nearly rolled back into her head. Her pussy was plumped and pouting. She'd creamed up well for them both and her clit was aroused and eager.

Killian spread her thighs and held them there forcibly at the knees, so she was completely spread out and exposed. He slipped between them and she felt his hot breath bathe her pussy. Killian groaned low in his throat as he licked from her anus to her clit over and over in mind-numbing strokes. Moira arched her back at the feel of his questing tongue teasing the aroused flesh of her sex. Her clit engorged and pulled from its hood.

Dain's head came down first on her mouth for a possessive kiss, which she returned near desperately, then he dipped down and pulled one of her nipples between his lips and sucked and laved. Moira closed her eyes and panted in pleasure at having both these men solely and completely focused on her body. To her there was no better sensation than the one she had right now. Dain's hand dipped down, brushing through her pubic hair to her sex. His fingers bumped into Killian as they each pleasured her. Dain rubbed his finger around her clit while Killian sucked her labia and stabbed his tongue up inside her.

Today they did not tease or deliberately hold off her climax. Today they both were focused utterly on the business at hand.

Moira writhed and arched her spine as she came explosively for them.

Killian thrust two fingers within her as Dain relentlessly teased her clit and her first climax rolled right into a second one.

Her body humming, she arched up, unable to take any more. "Please," she nearly sobbed. "I need to feel both of you." It was getting to the point she needed both their touches as much she needed air to breathe.

Keeping their gazes on her, both Dain and Killian disrobed. With every item of clothing cast aside, Moira felt needier.

Dain pulled her against him and kissed her. He ran his hands greedily over her body, teasing her nipples and dragging his fingers over her sex, pushing her once again to dance at the razor's edge of climax. Behind her, Killian pressed his body against her, delving his hand down between the cheeks of her buttocks to tease her anus and laying kisses on her shoulders and the nape of her neck.

Moira moaned low in her throat and turned over to face Killian. She kissed him hard and deep, aggressively stabbing her tongue into his mouth to taste him. He broke the kiss and arched his spine with a gasp when she found his cock and pumped him.

Moira nipped and licked her way down Killian's magnificent body and took his beautiful organ into her mouth. His breath hissed out of him at the contact and he buried his hands in her hair, his body going tense. She swirled her tongue around the smooth head, closing her eyes.

She loved taking both these men into her mouth as much they seemed to love licking her.

Behind her she felt Dain run his fingers over her pussy and tease her clit back and forth with the pad of one. He spread her labia and speared his tongue inside her, making her lose her pace on Killian's cock and moan around it.

Suddenly, she was hauled backward against Dain's chest. He dragged her up against him and parted her thighs, spreading her like a meal for Killian. Killian rose up between her legs, hungrily staring down at her swollen, dripping pussy.

"Take her," Dain rasped in a low voice. "I want to see you fuck her until she comes."

His voice rumbled through his chest and into her back, making her quake and shiver with need.

Killian rose up on his hands and knees, his eyes dark with passion. He ran a finger teasingly over her sex and Moira whimpered in the back of her throat. "You want me here?" he asked, his gaze holding hers. He slipped a finger inside her pussy and eased it in and out until she shuddered.

"Yes," she gasped.

He rubbed his finger around the entrance that seemed to open and close hungrily at his touch. Blessedly, he guided his cock inside. Killian threw back his head on a groan when he'd seated himself deep inside her. Moira arched her spine at the feel of him. He was much like his brother in all ways, though Killian was a little longer where Dain was a little wider.

Dain slid his hands up to caress her breasts and roll her nipples between his fingers. His chest was warm against her back and his hard cock stabbed into her lower back. "Is it good, Moira?" he asked near her ear, sending shivers down her spine. "Does he fill you well?"

"Yes," she murmured feverishly.

Killian set a slow and easy pace, thrusting into her with long, steady strokes. Moira writhed and tossed her head under the eroticism of having Dain hold her while Killian took her. It made her near insensible with excitement. Dain smoothed his hand up her body and toyed with her breasts and nipples, all the while murmuring in her ear about how excited she made him.

Killian picked up the pace, rocking his hips into her forcefully and spearing her to the base of his cock in each stroke. Moira came screaming in Dain's arms as Dain held her close.

"Yes, that's it, love," murmured Dain. "I love to watch you come."

She gripped Dain's legs, unable to respond in the final throes of her climax. Moira felt the muscles of her pussy grasp Killian's shaft tightly, milking him. Killian thrust deeply into her a final time and groaned as he released himself inside her.

As soon as the tremors had passed and she lay trembling under Killian's big body, Dain eased himself out from under her and sought something in the saddlebags. When he came back, she knew what he wanted. She got to her knees and offered herself up to him, desire already heating her blood at the thought of Dain within her. She would take him any way he wanted her. All she wanted was to maintain an intimate connection with him for as long as possible.

Killian came down on her side, panting hard. Idly he toyed with her breast, teasing her nipple as Dain coated himself in the oil and set the head of his cock to her anus. She tensed as she always tensed.

Dain reached up and gently smoothed her unbound hair away from her neck. "Hush. You know you're going to like it," he murmured.

Yes, she knew she would.

She bit her lip as he pushed the silky crown past the tight ring of nerves and closed her eyes. Killian watched as desire slackened her face and caressed her hanging breasts relentlessly.

Dain began to stroke into her body. She writhed beneath him, pushing back at him in order to drive him farther into her. He let out a deep groan and clamped his hands on her hips to hold her in place. With his strong grip he drove into her, making her gasp and claw the bedclothes.

Killian stroked his hands down her body as Dain pushed closer and closer to the edge of climax. He toyed with her nipples and stroked the pad of his finger over her swollen clit.

With Moira came it was in a screaming frenzy of sensation. She bucked beneath him and called Dain's name and Dain lost control. He pushed himself deep inside her and came.

Panting, sheened with perspiration and sated beyond all possible belief, Moira collapsed to the bed. She closed her eyes, feeling cool cloths on her body as they cleaned her, then the hard, warm press of their bodies on either side of her.

Dain pulled her close and kissed her temple. Killian snuggled up at her back. Moira fell asleep wrapped in deep contentment, her body and heart feeling well loved.

How could give this up?

But the end was near. She could feel it.

Chapter Nine

🕉

Dain had been to Sudhra many times and every time he liked it less.

When Sudhra had been a sovereign nation instead of a territory of New Ecasia, they'd been very intolerant of anyone who wasn't a male loyal in worship to the God Anot. Their views on sex were primitive. A man could commit adultery, but a woman who committed adultery would be punished by death. Though there had been a flourishing sex slave operation within the country that everyone knew about but no one was willing to openly acknowledge.

Women had been considered as property with no right to so much as speak before being spoken to. The noblewomen had had it much easier, but the lowborn, the women who'd made up the overwhelming majority of the female part of the population, their lives must've been something from the Underworld.

The echo of that culture persisted. It left an indelible imprint on a country so that even hundreds of years later the specter of the previous ways of being still tainted the land. Even though women now had rights equal to that of men in Sudhra, there remained a cloying, suffocating sense of inequality.

Sarar City was small and especially cloying. Worse, Dain could feel Cyric here.

He walked to the window of the small room he shared with Moira and pulled aside the gray linen curtains to gaze out into the small marketplace in the street below.

It had to be his imagination. He merely felt anxious at the prospect of seeing Cyric again. Surely that was the cause for the feeling of his rage brushing just under his skin like some wild cat trying to be shed of its cage. He couldn't allow that, but it had seemed a constant battle since they'd arrived to keep it tamped down, leashed within him.

His rage wanted release, focus.

Moira set her hand to his upper arm, startling him.

"I hate this place," he muttered. "It is so incredibly hot here. It feels like high summer when it should feel like spring."

She leaned against him and stared down at the dusty street where shopkeepers and traders were setting up for a market day. "We've gone through a drastic change of season in our travels, it's true."

To Dain, it seemed the seasons had changed overnight. This far south it was warm, too warm for his northern Aeolian blood. Flowers bloomed in profusion here, scenting the air with a sweetness that seemed so at odds with his feelings.

He drew Moira close and kissed the top of her head. The scent of her instantly tightened his body. Goddess, how the woman affected him. He cared for her...deeply. He wished he could keep her. As it was, they'd deal with Cyric and then part ways. It was the only way it could be. Dain just wanted her free of the psychic attacks. On the arduous journey to this place, she'd had three of them. Every one had nearly stopped his heart. It seemed the closer they got to Cyric the worse they'd become.

Perhaps when this was over and Moira was free of the attacks, free to continue on with her life, she and Killian would be able to find happiness together. Dain knew they each cared for the other and perhaps that caring would one day translate into love.

Dain's heart squeezed at the thought of losing her. How it would kill a part of his soul. He had no choice, however. He was far too dangerous a man for her to remain with, and if he had to lose her to someone better that it was his own brother. Dain knew that Killian would treat her the way Moira deserved to be treated.

She turned toward him and buried her face in his chest. "I cannot get enough of you, Dain," she whispered.

Ah, she read his mind. He couldn't get enough of her either. He closed his eyes briefly against a sharp pain that speared through his body at the thought of her loss.

"Thank you for coming with me. I know how hard this is for you," she continued.

If she only knew why.

Dain tipped her head to his and kissed her. Her lips felt so smooth and soft under his mouth. Her tongue against his made him hard. The taste of her fired his blood. He pushed himself against her stomach, letting her feel exactly what she did to him and she snaked her hand between their bodies to rub his shaft, making him groan.

They were both exhausted from the intense journey. They'd arrived the previous evening and had immediately rented rooms at a downtown inn. He, Killian, and Moira had sat up late for dinner and shared a bottle of expensive red wine in celebration of their arrival. Killian had drunk most of it. They'd slept soundly the night before, but were all still recovering from the previous night's festivities.

All the same, he wanted her as he always wanted her and it seemed she wanted him as well. She freed his already hard shaft from his trews and stroked the foreskin down.

Dain tangled his hands in her soft hair and drew her mouth to his for another kiss. She returned it hungrily, mating her tongue with his and sending ripples of arousal shooting up his spine. Her fingers danced over his cock, skillfully finding all the sweet spots he possessed. They'd come to know each other's bodies well in the way of lovers over the past couple of months.

Giving him a mischievous look, she sank down on her knees and licked around the head of his shaft. His hips jerked forward and he let out a hiss of breath between his clenched teeth. Moira took him into her mouth without any preamble and sucked, letting the head of his cock slip past her tonsils and down her throat.

Dain tipped his head back and groaned. He tightened his hands on her shoulders. She cupped and massaged his scrotum with one hand, while using the other to work the base of his shaft as she brought him in and out of her mouth with increasing speed, letting the head of his cock slide down her tight throat. The heat of her mouth made him crazy with the need to bury himself balls-deep within her sweet pussy.

She slipped him out of her mouth and ran her tongue just under the head of his cock, licking and sucking at the place directly below it where he was most sensitive.

Dain's body tensed, his fingers tangling in the hair at the back of her head. His hips moved forward as he thrust his cock into her mouth once, unable to hold himself back. She shot a smoldering look up at him as she teased him with the tip of her tongue.

And that was it. That was all he could handle.

He swooped her up and sat her on the edge of the nearby table, standing between her spread legs. He kissed her and then set his forehead to hers. "You are a witch, my little one. You tempt me beyond all possible control."

She smiled up him. "That was my objective, Dain."

He pulled her toward him, positioning her so her bottom was at just at the edge of the table and her legs dangled over the side on either side of his hips. He thrust her skirts of her nightgown up to her hips. The abrupt action wiped the smile off her face. Her pussy brushed his cock, and she moaned and wiggled her hips, trying to get some friction going. He snaked his hand between their bodies and rubbed her clit with the pad of his forefinger. It was already plumped and aroused.

He gave a little laugh. "Eager, are we?"

"For you, always," she said with a little gasp.

He pulled her nightgown over her head and threw it to the floor. Her nipples topped her lush breasts like small cherries. Every time he saw her naked her beauty made his heart skip a beat. He caught her breasts against his palms and laved over each excited nipple in turn until she moaned for him. "Brace your hands behind you on the table, so your lovely breasts are bared for me."

He stood back and drank in his fill of her. In this position, her breasts were thrust forward in erotic offering. Her sex was excited and plumped, slicked with cream that made it glisten. "How do you feel right now, Moira?" he asked in a low voice.

Her breath came fast. "Excited, vulnerable…impatient."

He gave another low laugh and stepped toward her. His hand went to her pussy, and he slipped his fingers over and around the slick folds of her labia, using her moisture to bathe her distended clit. His finger slipped around the excited knot of nerves and it grew even larger under his ministrations. She whimpered and moved her hips forward, as if looking for something to fill her.

Dain slipped his finger down teasingly slowly and slid it into her hot, tight little slit. A feral-sounding moan ripped from Moira's throat and her back arched. He added a second, stretching her muscles further, and thrust in and out.

"Oh, sweet Goddess," she breathed, closing her eyes. "You know exactly what I love, Dain."

157

He growled low. "Like this?" He found her pleasure point and rubbed his fingertips over it. "Do you like this?"

Moira bucked and moaned under the influence of his fingers working her. His thumb went to her clit and circled it around and around. She climaxed long and hard. Her muscles clenched around his fingers and she cried out his name.

He removed his hand and set his cock to her entrance. "My name sounds so sweet on your lips, Moira," he purred.

She pushed her hips forward so the very tip of him barely entered her and she rocked her hips. "Please, Dain. Give me more," she whispered hoarsely.

Inch by inch he entered her, feeling her slick, hot pussy enclose his cock like a perfectly fitted glove. Finally, he was sheathed within her to the base of his cock.

"You are the tightest, silkiest woman I ever felt around my cock, Moira," he said with a shudder. Lowering his mouth to her breast with a growl, he took a nipple into his mouth and laved it with his tongue. At the same time, he pressed his hands to her buttocks and began to thrust in and out of her.

Moira climaxed again and her vaginal muscles convulsed around his length, making Dain groan around her nipple. He pumped into her relentlessly harder and faster until Moira was keening. He pushed her to yet another orgasm, and he came with a bellow, bathing her womb deep inside with his seed. Pleasure enveloped his body, driving him higher and higher. He grabbed onto her and buried his face in her throat to breathe in the sweet scent of her skin. The waves of climax eased, leaving him relaxed and sated.

Moira wrapped her arms around him and they stayed connected at the pelvis. Together they clung, breathing hard. Dain closed his eyes and enjoyed the feel of her around and against his body, the scent of her in his nostrils and the sound of her breathing harsh yet soft in his ears.

He raised his head and kissed her lingeringly. "I love you, Moira," he murmured.

Her body went stiff.

The words had come out of his mouth without him even knowing it. He didn't regret saying them. It was true. He loved Moira more than he'd even loved any woman.

"Dain," she murmured back. "I love you too. Goddess," her voice broke, "so much."

He laid a hand to her cheek. How he wanted to keep her. "I love you Moira, with everything I am, but you must know that—"

She shook her head. "Let's not speak of it now, Dain. Can we...can we just for one day pretend there is nothing that comes between us?"

He stood looking down at her. One day he would explain to her that it was because he loved her that they couldn't be together...but not today. Today Moira could have any manner of fiction from him that she wished.

Someone knocked on the door. He scooped up Moira's nightgown and she slid it over her head as he did up his trews. "Come in," Dain called.

Killian poked his head into the room. "You two are loud enough to wake the entire inn," he complained.

Dain laughed. "Too much wine last night, Killian?"

Killian just waved him off. "I'm going back to bed," he grumbled as he shut the door.

* * * * *

Moira squeezed Dain's hand, happy to simply be touching him. Today they would enjoy this small city and recover from their incredibly hard journey from the Port of Paradise. If she were to look at a map of New Ecasia, she could find Aeoli at its northernmost tip and this city at its southernmost tip. It was as if Cyric had gone as far as he could without leaving the country to get away from Dain.

Deep in thought, she stopped in front of a jewelry merchant and examined a small silver pendant depicting an owl with outspread wings. It reminded her of the times she'd seen Dain swooping over the castle tower at Aeodan with his huge white owl's wings spread. She smoothed her thumb over it, smiling at the memory.

Before she even realized he'd done it, Dain had purchased the necklace and was fastening it around her throat. "Dain," she said, fingering the charm. "I saw the tag. That was a very ex—"

"Shhh." He took her hand and they melded back into the crowd. "It looks beautiful on you."

They bought a couple of fruit pies and nibbled them as they walked through the market examining the wares. For the first time in a very long time, Moira relaxed. She allowed herself to feel happiness and contentment, without any thought of the future. She slipped her hand into Dain's and smiled at him. He smiled back and leaned in to give her small kiss on the lips. The kiss of a couple long accustomed to touching, sharing their bodies. An easy kiss of committed love.

Emotion caught in her throat. Joy swelled in her chest.

It was then she felt the psychic tug.

She stopped in the middle of the thoroughfare, making the crowd part to flow around her. Dain had wandered to the side to examine some silver daggers. Moira felt the tug again. This time a flash of Cyric's face accompanied it. Could it be he was in the market somewhere?

She bit her lower lip, glancing at Dain. He was busy negotiating a price for a dagger and waist holster, probably one to replace hers. He'd mentioned he'd wanted to buy her them when they'd left that morning. If it was Cyric somehow drawing her now, it would be better if Dain was perhaps not around to meet him. She felt she owed it Dain to keep him out of this situation as much as possible. She understood well that he wanted no part of Cyric H'valvric.

She walked over to him and touched his arm, interrupting his bickering with the merchant. "I'll be three stalls down looking at fabric," she said.

He kissed her quickly. "I'll meet you there."

Feeling intensely guilty about her lie, she let the crowd engulf her. It was for the best, she assured herself. She wanted to protect Dain as much as possible.

Moira slipped between a silk vendor and a fruit merchant. The fruit merchant nudged her as she passed. "Fresh apples," the woman enticed. "Shiny and juicy, straight from apple orchards of Mid-Nordan."

She shook her head and continued on, feeling that tendril of magick teasing her, pulling at her. Moira made her way through the throng of people, following after it. It led her down a semi-busy street, then down another less busy one. Finally, down a side alley.

She stopped at the mouth of the street, wondering if she'd chased a ghost. A flicker of black passed the opposite end of the alley and it spurred her on. The alley opened up into a huge manicured courtyard. A large house with tall golden columns graced the large front porch. Moira raised an eyebrow. Someone certainly thought a lot of themselves to have such a home built. Was it Cyric?

She stood in the shadows for several minutes, watching the house. Her best course of action was to find out who owned the property. She'd walked right up to Dain's front gates and had been frightened almost right out of her skin. In this situation her sixth sense told her to proceed more cautiously.

Moira went stiff, sensing the presence of people around her.

She turned to come back the way she'd come and ran straight into a broad chest. Moira looked up into the face of a grizzled-faced man. He grabbed her by the upper arms. "Lord Cyric's been expecting you," the man said and started dragging her toward the house.

Panic overwhelmed her for a moment, then a primal reaction kicked in. She stomped on the man's foot and when he cried out in surprise and pain, she wrenched her arm free of him and ran for the alley...only to have two more men block her path. Moira stopped short and glanced around wildly, looking for another way out of the courtyard.

"I knew you were here, Moira," said a baritone voice behind her. "I sent the men to bring you to talk with me."

Slowly, she turned and saw Cyric standing in front of his door.

"Come on." He motioned with his hand. "I won't hurt you." He turned and walked back into his house.

There was that tendril of magick again, pulling at her, tugging her toward Cyric.

Curious and beckoned by forces unseen, she followed him.

Chapter Ten

ॐ

"Killian!"

Killian woke to a hard shake of his shoulder. "Ugh!" was all he could say as the force the drinking binge he'd engaged in the night before came crashing down on his head. "Great Goddess, Dain. You and Moira are making enough noise for a whole lifetime today."

"She's gone," Dain said, flopping down on the bed beside him. "I've looked all morning for her. She just disappeared."

Killian sat up and ran a hand through his hair. His head pounded out a beat in time to the sudden thump of his heart. "What do you mean Moira's gone?" he asked slowly.

"We were in the market. She told me she'd meet me a few stalls down, but she wasn't there." Dain stood. "Come on, we've got to find her."

His brother's voice held a very definite note of anger and fear. Killian knew how much he'd come to care for Moira. Dain would never forgive himself if something happened to her.

Killian stood carefully and reached for his clothing. "Just relax, Dain. This is small city. She can't be far."

"Yes, but Cyric is here," Dain replied in a flat voice.

Killian paused a moment as he pulled his shirt over his head. "I know."

* * * * *

Moira walked into a lavishly decorated parlor. Antique furniture, dating from before the Sudhraian–Nordanese war, if Moira was not mistaken, decorated the large room. Dark red silk drapes covered the windows, making the room dark. It smelled heavily of the lilies that seemed to sit in colorful vases on every possible surface.

"Come in," said Cyric. "Have a seat." He motioned toward an uncomfortable straight-backed chair.

The magick pulled her forward into the room. She raised her eyes from the chair to Cyric and the knowledge slammed into her. The magick didn't emanate from her as she'd originally thought.

It came from him.

"You," she breathed. "You're magicked."

Cyric's shapely mouth broke into a wide smile. "It took you this long to feel it? It must be because I'm holding my power back. Here, let me help you to understand."

Another magickal force rose in the room. It brushed against her magick, pushed at it. A strange pulsing vibration darkened through her. Moira lost her breath for a moment. "Darkened through her" was the only way to describe the short, violent burst of power. It clashed with her own magick, warring with it briefly before retreating.

Then another burst of power hit her. She felt it push at her once, then *punch*. Moira fell backward, sprawling on the carpet behind her. Pain burst through her stomach and she closed her eyes, fighting through it as nausea overwhelmed her. The power receded, leaving her feeling weak.

She looked up at Cyric through the tangle of her hair, realizing with trepidation how much more powerful Cyric was than she.

Cyric smiled.

"You've come earlier than I expected." He sounded as sated as a snake that had just swallowed a kitten. "I knew you'd come, just didn't expect you so soon."

"How do you know who I am?" Cold rage put a hard edge in her voice.

"Precognitive ability, my girl. I saw you and your boyfriends coming a long time ago."

"Why do you care who I am? I have no connection to you."

Cyric walked toward her and knelt. He inhaled near her hair. "You stink of both of them, but mostly of Dain." Cyric sneered his name. "I'm an Aviat, too, Moira. I have an excellent sense of smell and I can scent that you've slept with both them...repeatedly." He gave a short malicious laugh. "You've fallen in love with Dain, at least, of course. All the women do. You came here without either of them, didn't you?" His tone was one of wonder. "You're either brave or incredibly stupid. I'm going to bet on the latter."

Rage made her entire body tremble. "You haven't answered my question."

Cyric smiled. "You've become the d'Ange brothers' little whore." His voice was the softest caress. "I find that incredibly intriguing."

Her hair was long and tangled, obscuring her vision of Cyric's face. She met his gaze, filled with the knowledge that she might die. Moira shifted to her other side, feigning discomfort and sought the dagger sheathed in the holster at her side. Her fingers curled around the handle. "Dain never killed his wife," she said with certainty. "You did."

He only laughed. "Believe what you like. Love is always so blind. You love him so much that the reason you came here alone was to save him from having to face me, wasn't it? How valiant."

She pulled the dagger and flew up at him, landing a hard and deep slash to his chest. Blood welled through his white linen shirt. Cyric yelled in surprise and rolled to the side.

Moira lunged to her feet and ran for the door. Dagger still in hand, she threw it open and felt the glorious light of freedom on her face...right before a meaty hand closed around her shoulder and spun her around.

The guards from the courtyard.

She fought like something wild, kicking and screaming and biting. She went for the throat and the eyes, hearing satisfying yelps of pain. Two men grabbed her, one for each arm. One of them closed his hand around the wrist that held the dagger and squeezed. Pain blossomed up the length of her arm into her shoulder, but she didn't relinquish her blade.

The guard's enormous hand grasped the hair at the back of her head and Cyric's face filled her vision. She struggled against the guard and only succeeded in ripping out some of her own hair.

"Let. It. Go," the guard snarled. He bit her palm and she yelped and opened her hand. The blade fell to the foyer floor.

She looked up, her gaze focusing on Cyric. Death shone in his eyes as he stalked toward her. Blood smeared the front of his expensive shirt.

Cyric clucked his tongue. Moira was getting tired of hearing that sound. "You're incredibly powerful and you don't even know it. You haven't even tried to harness your magick." He cocked his head to the side. "Or are you afraid of your abilities?"

Moira stilled for a moment, considering his words. Did he mean use her magick in her defense? Use it with the intention of harming someone?

Cyric laughed. "I can see it has never even occurred to you."

Moira struggled in the guards' embrace. "What do you want with me?" she demanded to know angrily.

"I should be the one asking that question. You're the one who sought me out."

She stilled. "Yes. Yes, that's true." She leveled her gaze at him. "To talk. Nothing else."

"Talk about what? What shall I talk of with the lover of my worst enemy?"

She shook her head. "I don't know. I've been led to you for some reason beyond this world. The Goddess and the God manipulated me into seeking first Dain and then you. I don't know why."

"Hmmm." Cyric stroked his chin thoughtfully. "Take her to my bedroom."

His bedroom? Alarms rang through her head. She struggled even harder against the guards as they bore her out of the room and down the hallway. The guards opened a door and threw her into a large bedchamber. She landed on her side on the carpet and bounded to her feet, only to find herself able to pound on the already closed and locked door. She pulled at the doorknob and hit it with her closed fists, letting her rage spill out of her. Her magick flared within her hard and hot.

Finally, she turned and glanced around the chamber, taking in the ornate carved wooden bed, the wardrobes and tables and chairs. The room was enormous.

There were no windows. There were no other doors that she could see, either.

No possible immediate means of escape apparent, she launched herself from where she leaned against the door and started going through the wardrobes and dressers, searching for something she could use as a weapon. Moira pulled Cyric's clothing out and tossed it to the ground, scattered his shoes, but could find nothing to use as a weapon. They'd obviously swept the room clean before they'd thrown her into it.

Dejected and desolate, she sat down on one of the fine rugs that covered the floor in the middle of the mess she'd made. Looking up, she spotted the perfect thing. Next to the hearth was a fire poker. How could they have missed such a thing? She scrambled over and took it from its place in the fire tool holder. The cold metal felt strong in her hands and gave her a measure of confidence.

You're incredibly powerful and you don't even know it. Cyric's words echoed in her mind. Magick as a weapon? She bit her lip and stared down at the poker. Perhaps.

Tears pricked her eyes. One plopped down into her lap, splashing on the back of her hand. She didn't cry because she was frightened for herself. She cried for Dain. Cyric had not admitted it, but she knew it in her heart. Cyric's magick had killed Andreea.

Dain had been punishing himself for nothing.

That is what The Powers had wanted her to discover. That was the purpose to all her attacks, to everything. She'd been meant to clear Dain of wrongdoing and free him from the prison he'd locked himself in. She gripped the poker harder. There was no way she wasn't going to get out of here and tell Dain that he was innocent.

Magick as a weapon...

Moira closed her eyes and found the thread of magick that was interwoven with her soul. She could feel it at times, shining like a golden lifeline within her, but she'd never consciously sought it out.

It was time she found out how strong she truly was.

Chapter Eleven

ꙮ

Dain gritted his teeth as Cyric's house came into view. It was set back from the main part of the town and as soon as he saw it, he figured Lord Cyric all but ruled this small city. The house was more like a castle and no expense had been spared to ensure all the viewers knew how powerful and wealthy Cyric was.

Dain shared a look with Killian and they moved toward it, thankful for the cover of night.

* * * * *

As soon as Moira heard footsteps on the opposite side of the door, she scrambled to hide herself on the side of it.

"Liiiittle laaaaady," called one of the guards in heavily accented Nordanese. The door opened slowly. "Liiiittle…oof!"

Moira brought the poker hard straight into the man's gullet, then brought it down again over his head. She winced and tried not to scream as she did it. Never in her life had her hands been the cause of violence, only healing, but she had no time to be regretful and squeamish now.

The guard slumped to his knees in front of her, unconscious. Blood trickled from his forehead. The tray he'd been carrying crashed to the carpet, making far more noise than she wanted.

She dropped the poker to the carpeted floor and quickly plucked the man's short sword and dagger from his side. With trembling fingers, she pushed the dagger into the waistband of her skirts and clutched the sword's sheath in her hand. Feet silent on the thick carpet, she inched toward the doorway, peered out to make sure no one was there and then slinked down the corridor toward the main part of the house.

She frowned as she passed a mahogany table with a gold vase of flowers on it. That hadn't been there before, she was sure. And the picture of the sunset on the opposite wall, that hadn't been there either.

Something was wrong.

Once she made her first left, she knew there *was* something terribly, *terribly* wrong. She had paid attention when the guards had been hauling her to the room. Every turn they'd made, she'd documented carefully and remembered so that she could find her way back out. But it seemed the house had somehow shifted and changed.

She turned right and came to a dead end. She huffed out an impatient breath and turned to retreat the way she'd come. She *knew* she hadn't forgotten the way. There had to be another explanation and Moira felt sure she wasn't going to like it.

Finding a small alcove the Sudhraians seemed fond of putting in their homes, she closed her eyes, searching for a thread of her magick. She found a tendril curling through her and grabbed it. Never had she harnessed her magick deliberately before. It had always come to the fore naturally. Now she would try to apply it to this house in order to discover its secrets.

And hopefully find a way out to Dain and Killian.

* * * * *

Killian and Dain were desperately searching for a way in to get to Moira.

Killian watched his brother disappear around a corner of the house only to come back with a grim expression on his face. "I swear there was a window there before," Dain growled, a muscle working in his jaw. "The front door has disappeared now, too."

"This house is heavily magicked, brother," Killian said, looking up at the massive structure. He lowered his gaze to Dain. "Did you know that Cyric was a descendant of the First Children?"

Dain gave his head a sharp shake. Moonlight showed a sharp flare of something across his face. Hope, perhaps? Killian knew he, himself, had hope burning his chest right now. If Cyric had magick, it meant there was a possibility that Dain hadn't killed Andreea after all.

"Perhaps he has a pet mage," Dain said in a flat tone.

"Perhaps. We won't know until we can get inside and find out what's going on."

* * * * *

Moira propelled the thread of her magick out and instantly felt it hit a tall potent wall of power. Her breath huffed out of her at the sensation. She feared Cyric might be able to sense what she was doing.

Ignoring the possibility since she had no other choice but to try, she opened her eyes and thrust her whole awareness out to the house, feeling it as though it were a living thing. The falseness of it hit her first. She scowled, feeling the strangeness of the structure. It felt *off*. She pulsed her magick at it, feeling something in her chest begin to grow warm. She pressed her palm between her breasts at the not-unpleasant feeling.

"Show me the truth," she murmured.

She gasped as the air before her shimmered once, twice. She closed her eyes for a moment against dizziness and when she opened them, the house she remembered was now back in place. Frowning, she glanced to her right and saw the room which she'd first entered. Perhaps she'd released the spell of illusion that had been over the house?

Oh, sweet Goddess. Cyric would know she'd done that for certain.

Panic surged through her veins. She inched out of the alcove and kept close to the wall, making straight for the door.

Cyric stepped from the shadows opposite her and grabbed her throat. She gasped and choked. He pushed her back against the wall behind her, his grip still crushing her windpipe. She tried to pry his fingers loose, but his hold was like steel.

He lifted a brow and smiled. "Going somewhere?"

Regaining her presence of mind, she remembered her weapon. She slid the sheath from the short sword and swiped toward him. Cyric released her and jumped back just in time. The very tip of the sword sliced through his white linen shirt and Cyric's blood welled from his abdomen. He stared down at the wound in surprise.

That was twice she'd blooded him, she thought with satisfaction.

Eyes wide and breathing heavy, Moira whirled and ran for the door. Before she'd taken five steps, a thick, heavy magickal rope seemed to wrap itself around her. It tripped her and she fell face-forward onto the tiled floor. The short sword flew from her hand and slid across the foyer.

She sent her magick to the ropes to try and undo them. She pushed and pulled at Cyric's magick frantically, hearing his boot falls on the floor coming nearer and nearer.

Finally, she broke his hold and turned over to face him, rage heating her blood to a boiling point. With her emotion, she felt her magick rise. She'd never known she could use her magick in a battle this way...and it felt *good* to harness its power.

A slow smiled bloomed on Cyric's thin lips. "You found the weapon I left you in the room, I see. I wanted to see what you'd do to try and escape." His eyes darkened and his smile faded. "But I never imagined you'd be able to undo the illusion cloaking the house."

She sought the dagger hidden in the folds of her skirts. To her left, she felt the presence of two men she recognized. She breathed a sigh of relief. "You," she ground out at Cyric. "You're the cause of all Dain's pain."

He shrugged. "Andreea wanted to cease our relationship when Dain came back. I was angry."

"Was it intentional?"

A slow smile bloomed on Cyric's thin lips. "Of course. Making it appear Dain had done it was a stroke of genius. He has no magick, by the way. The imbecile."

Her magick flared within her and threatened to boil over. She tamped it down with effort, controlling it, focusing it. Cyric's magick swelled and pushed against her, rubbing against hers.

Death rasped against life. Putrefaction abraded with purification.

"So now he knows," she said with satisfaction.

He laughed. "He'll never know because the information will die with you." He lunged at her. She brought her dagger to stab him in the chest, but suddenly he was simply...gone. Dain had bolted from the shadows and hit him from the side. Together he and Cyric rolled across the tile floor.

Moira winced, watching them surge to their feet and punch each other. Cyric kicked Dain in the head and Dain staggered back, dazed.

Killian ran into the fray, sword raised, but Cyric wrapped his magick around him, holding him in place. Cyric took that moment to raise his hand and Moira felt his magick coalesce. It grew dark and powerful. *Lethal.*

She closed her eyes and pointed her magick at him with the goal of stripping him of his. Her own instincts guided her now and nothing more. Moira pulled her power into the center of her chest, molding and strengthening it.

Cyric took notice of her and she felt part of his power lift its head like some great cat and stare at her.

Moira opened her eyes and let her power surge forth. It poured out of her like a tidal wave. She screamed at its release and the ripping pain that accompanied it.

Cyric cried out, stepping back and warding himself against the burst of power.

"I grasp your power and expel it!" she yelled at the top of her lungs.

She felt something break free of Cyric and release upward. The very air around them swelled to near bursting and then collapsed in on itself. An ear-shattering rushing sound filled the room.

"No!" Cyric screamed in anguish. The dark, heavy power that had previously filled the room dissipated.

Killian collapsed to his knees, freed.

Moira pushed to her feet, her head pounding. She had expelled everything she had in order to rip Cyric's magick from him and throw it to the four corners of the world. Dark spots appeared in her vision and she gasped, collapsed to the floor and tumbled into nothingness.

Chapter Twelve

ຂວ

"Moira," Dain yelled. He stepped toward her, but Cyric blocked his way. Fury bubbled up within him powerfully, as hard and as fast as it had when he'd come home from the war and found Cyric fucking his wife.

But this time he knew he had no killing magick to accompany it. He narrowed his eyes.

He only had his blade.

Dain stepped back and drew his sword from its scabbard. He stood in battle stance and brandished it at Cyric. His voice shook with absolute, cold rage when he spoke. "He's mine, Killian. Stay back. *Cyric, draw your sword.*"

Cyric glanced down at Moira and clucked his tongue. "At least I have the satisfaction of knowing that the stripping of my magick killed her. The weak little chit."

"*Draw your sword,*" Dain bellowed.

"That's two of your bed partners I've killed now, isn't it, Dain?"

He hefted his blade and ran at Cyric, but Cyric drew his sword and stepped out of Dain's way. Cyric brought his own sword around with the intention of taking Dain from behind, but Dain turned just in time to block Cyric's downward stroke.

Dain chastised himself for allowing Cyric to manipulate his emotions and make him lose control. He fought hard for a measure of neutrality, a place where he could fight with an uncluttered mind. Dain drew in a breath and swung his sword at his opponent's midsection but Cyric caught his blade mid-blow, causing their swords to scrape against one another. The lengths kissed as Cyric managed to push Dain up against the wall, bringing his blade dangerously close to his throat. Cyric's stale breath teased his nostrils.

Dain was unconcerned. Cyric might've had strong magick...but there was *no way* he was going to beat him blade to blade.

In his peripheral vision he saw Killian stalk toward them, sword raised. Dain stared into Cyric's black eyes as he commanded in a low voice, "This is my revenge, Killian. Stay out of it. I've got him right where I want him."

"Uh, you do?"

Dain hooked his foot around Cyric's ankles and swept, sending him crashing down beneath him. Cyric's sword clattered to the stone floor beside him and Dain brought his own sword straight down into his chest without fanfare, without preamble.

"Yes, I do," Dain said as he stared down into Cyric's surprised eyes. "That was for Andreea and Moira." He twisted the blade and pulled it from Cyric's body.

Cyric stared up at him with a stunned look on his face. He gargled once and blood trailed from the corner of his mouth, then the light in his eyes went out.

Dain let his sword clatter to the floor and ran to Moira. Killian was already there. Dain knelt beside her, emotion welling up within him. If she was truly dead, he didn't know what he'd do. He took her in his arms, noticing a bruise on her forehead and a cut on her lip. Her head fell back, exposing her slender throat and the fine blue veins that marked it.

"Anot's blood," Killian breathed. He leaned down and pressed his hand to her throat. "She's alive, though only barely."

Hope flared hot and hard within him. Dain crushed her to him and closed his eyes, inhaling the fresh scent of her hair. Then he lifted her and walked toward the door. "Let's get her back to the room."

* * * * *

Moira came awake lying comfortably in the bed at the inn. Someone had covered her with a sheet, but nothing more because of the heat. Her head ached and her body felt sore, but otherwise she felt fine. The last thing she remembered was ripping Cyric's magick away from him. Suddenly concerned she'd ripped her own away in the process, she closed her eyes and sought the threads of her power.

She sighed. They were still there, diminished and weak from the exertion, but they were there.

Murmurings drew her gaze up. Dain and Killian stood at the window looking out at the street. She smiled, knowing in her heart that Cyric had been vanquished from their lives forever. She let her gaze travel over them lovingly. How she cared for them both. The emotion she felt for them was different, but intense in each individual way. The feelings she had made her heart swell and tears prick her eyes.

Killian she loved for his easy laughter and gentle ways. She loved how he loved his brother and how he'd do anything for him. In that, they had much in common. She loved the way he touched her body in an almost reverent way and the darkness that filled his eyes when he was aroused to the point of breaking.

Dain. Her eyes filled with tears. *Goddess, how she loved him*. Loved him for his intensity, his honor, and his single-minded purpose in everything he did. Loved how he looked at her with so much caring in his eyes. Loved how he touched her and made fire erupt throughout her body. She loved the smell of him and the taste of him. He'd come to fill a part of her she hadn't even known had been empty. If she had to part with him, she didn't know if her heart could stand it.

Dain turned from the window and they locked gazes. His hair was unkempt and dark circles marked the skin beneath his eyes. She smiled.

"She's awake," he said in a hoarse, strained voice and came toward her.

Killian turned from the window. A smile spread over his lips. "Moira," he murmured.

Dain caught her up gently in his arms and scattered kisses over her forehead and cheeks and mouth. Then he held her close and murmured into her hair, "I thought you were going to leave me."

She wrapped her arms around him and closed her eyes. "Never," she whispered.

Dain eased her back into the pillows and Killian caught her hand, then leaned in and kissed her. "Cyric will bother us no more," he whispered against her mouth.

She nodded.

"How do you feel?" said Killian, settling in beside her.

"I feel like someone hit me with a shovel," she replied. "How long was I unconscious?"

"About twelve hours," Dain said. "The doctor came by and treated your injuries, but told us we could do nothing more than wait for you to awaken. We feared you never would."

She reached up and cupped his cheek in her hand, holding his gaze. Moira put everything she felt for him into her gaze and she saw the hint of tears fill Dain's eyes.

Killian cleared his throat, kissed her forehead and rose. "Well, now that this nasty business is concluded, I'm going to be on my way."

"Where are you going, Killian?" Moira asked.

"I thought I'd leave this afternoon. Maybe head back to Lord Arvand's court for a while and leave you two some time alone. I assume you'll be heading back to Aeodan as soon as Moira is ready?"

"We will, Killian," Dain answered. "We'll see you there." He stood and the brothers embraced. "Travel carefully."

"You too."

"Goodbye, Moira." Killian winked. "Take care of my brother. He loves you very much."

She smiled. "As I love him. Safe travels, Killian," she replied.

Killian laid a long, lingering kiss to her lips, a kiss of more than just a simple goodbye, and left the room. Moira stared at the door, wistful happiness threading through her body.

Dain brought a plate with some bread and cheese on it and tall glass of water. Moira pushed up carefully. Her stomach already rumbled at the sight of the food.

Dain pushed her hair away from her face. "As soon as you're ready to travel, I know a place not far from here where we can stay by the ocean and walk on the beach. Would you like to spend some time there? It is warm enough that we can swim in the water."

"Dain, yes. I would love that." She smiled broadly, just thinking of her feet sinking into the sand and the water lapping at her toes. Thinking of Dain at her side while she experienced those things made it even better.

"And then, when you've had enough of sun and sand, we can go home to Aeodan…together," he said.

She leaned forward and kissed him, then murmured huskily against his lips, "Nothing in this world could sound finer."

COMING TO A BOOKSTORE NEAR YOU!

ELLORA'S CAVE

Bestselling Authors Tour

Enjoy the following excerpts from:
AND LADY MAKES THREE

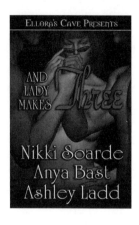

Featuring

PRISM *by NIKKI SOARDE*

TWILIGHT *by ANYA BAST*

PIRATE'S BOOTY *by ASHLEY LADD*

All Rights Reserved, Ellora's Cave Publishing, Inc.

PRISM

Copyright © NIKKI SOARDE, 2005.

He breathed a sigh of relief, and flopped back on the pillows. He hadn't slept as long as he thought, and still had an hour before he was due down at the Audi dealership. He was just mulling over the clients he was scheduled to see that afternoon when a loud snort from the other side of the bed demanded his attention.

He propped himself up on his elbow and looked down at the man beside him. He smiled and shook his head. Dax slept like he did everything—with gusto. His long wavy hair was fanned out across the pillow, his arms and legs flung wide. He had a knack for taking up almost three quarters of the available space on the bed, and his snores could rattle the windows at fifty paces. He worked hard, and played harder, his rugged physique and deeply bronzed skin, attesting to just how much time and energy he devoted to his passions. He gave his all in every situation, and he never turned his back on trouble. Or on a friend.

Barring the occasional forgivable one-night stand, and one catastrophic stab at the suburban white-picket-fence myth, Dax and Clay had been together almost since graduation and Clay had never once regretted his decision. They were good together. They were good friends, and God knew the sex was great.

So what was going wrong?

Clay knew he'd overreacted the night before, but he didn't know why. He also didn't know why they'd been arguing more lately, picking fights over everything from which brand of coffee they should buy to escalating long distance bills.

He lay back on the pillow and stared at the ceiling as he considered the events of the past few months. Had something changed and they just couldn't see it? If so, how did they figure out what *it* was, and when they did, what did they do about it?

But the more he thought about it, the more certain he was that *nothing* had changed.

Everything in their relationship was exactly the same as it had been a year ago. Two years ago. *Five* years ago.

And then it hit him. At last he knew exactly what was wrong. How could they have missed it? How could they have been so blind?

He closed his eyes and groaned. Now, if only he could figure out what to do about it.

TWILIGHT

"Are you all right this morning?" Dai asked. Her moods seemed so unknowable. He felt like he was constantly dancing on the edge of her temper.

"I-I'm fine" She shot him a glance. "I'm just fine."

He waited a heartbeat and then knelt beside her. "I think not. Tell me what is troubling you."

She turned to him. "*Why* could I feel you coming down that path? Why can I sense you in ways I've never been able to sense other people before?"

"I think you know the answer to that."

She sighed, stood, and walked to the tree line. He followed. Twyla whirled on him. "What do you two want from me?" Tears stood her eyes.

"You know the answer to that, too."

"You both want my body."

"Your body, yes. We're healthy males who have waited a long time for you. That goes without saying, but we want more than just your body."

"What, then? You want my emotion, my love, my-my *soul*?"

Dai smiled and shook his head. "Nico and I already have your soul, love. It's already intertwined with ours. We want the rest, though. Most of all, we want your love, freely given."

She stood there, looking up at him with large, tear-filled eyes. The way she looked now, she could almost fool him into thinking she was vulnerable. Maybe she was. He took a step toward her, wanting nothing more than to pull her into the circle of his arms and hold her.

"I don't have any love left to give," she whispered hoarsely and turned away from him.

He reached out and touched her shoulder. When she didn't jerk away, he pulled her to his chest and wrapped her in his arms. She let out a long, ragged sigh and relaxed against him. Closing his eyes, Dai inhaled the scent of her. His heart sung. To have her in his arms was better than all his imaginings. "You do," he murmured insistently into her hair. "Let Nico and I show you."

She turned in the circle of his embrace and tipped her face up toward his. Tears made tracks down her cheeks. "Kiss me," she whispered.

PIRATE'S BOOTY

Copyright © ASHLEY LADD, 2005.

Keir's warm breath tickled her neck. "Something troubling you, Princess?"

Her hand grasped her throat in shocked alarm.

"I have a name. Would it hurt you so terribly to use it?" She exhaled slowly as she turned to find him barely kissing distance away. Lifting her lashes slowly, she gazed up at him. Not as tall as his colleague, he was the perfect height, his nose level with the top of her head. His lips rested at her eye-level and from this distance, they looked ideal, too. Usually, she couldn't see them for his full beard, but at this distance, she could see them very clearly.

"Melena." Keir caressed her name as no other had before him. It rolled off his tongue like the richest Synkethian milk chocolate.

Mesmerized by his dark, sultry voice, a minute gasp escaped her lips. Quivers of lust racked her, and a strange twinge resounded between her legs. It might not hurt him terribly to use her given name, but apparently it made her ache. But it was too late to take it back now.

Realizing she stared as if he were her last supper, she cursed silently and forced herself to act nonchalant. She was chained by a thousand different prisons and had no right to quiver at his nearness or devour his lips with her gaze. Too late to act as if everything was sunny when she probably looked as if she were about to go nova so she confessed to the partial truth. At least, he wouldn't hear a lie in her voice. "What if we're never rescued?"

Swallowing the lump in her throat, she swept her gaze wide in an all-encompassing arc around the glade where they'd moved their camp. Lifting her chin high, she tried to sound confident, but her voice emerged strangled. "What if we spend the rest of our days on this planet, completely alone, except for the three of us?"

Keir raised his hand as if to stroke away the stray wisps of hair from her heated face, but it hovered mid-air and then dropped limply to his side. "We have to be optimistic. We can't give up hope."

If it were only the two of them, she and Keir, it could be paradise. But three? She worried her bottom lip between her teeth. Someone would be the odd man out and that spelled trouble.

Uncomfortably hot, bored, and frustrated, she glared. "Why? Shouldn't they have found us by now if they were searching? My people must think me dead from the explosion. They may not have launched any missions of rescue."

Keir slid a finger under her chin and forced her to look him square in the eye. His were deep, murky pools that she could happily drown in. "Because we'll go crazy if we give up. Because you're much stronger than that. We're not just going to lie down and die…"

Enjoy the following excerpts from:
Ellora's Cavemen:
Dreams of the Oasis I
Featuring:
Myla Jackson, Liddy Midnight, Nicole Austin, Allyson James, Paige Cuccaro, Jory Strong

A special edition anthology of six sizzling stories
from Ellora's Cave's Mistresses of Romantica.
Edited by Raelene Gorlinsky

THE AMBASSADOR'S WIDOW

Copyright © MYLA JACKSON, 2006.

"Okay, give me everything you've got." Andre settled in his seat on the small Lear jet blasting through the sky en route to Padel. Having showered at the hangar, he wore sweats and a T-shirt, preferring to make the transformation in clothing that didn't bind and had a little give.

Sean O'Banion leaned over Andre and pressed a button on the panel above him. A computer screen dropped down and blinked to life. "Here's all the footage we could muster on the man and we provided notes from one of our operatives on the inside."

"What about DNA?"

Melody handed him a jacket with several brown hairs scattered across the shoulders. "Try this. It was the jacket they found on him when he died."

Andre turned the jacket over. Armani. The guy had taste.

"No one saw him croak but our operative. We think we got him out in time, the press didn't get wind."

Andre knew how the agency worked. The less the press knew, the more easily a Chameleon blended in.

"For now." Melody sat in the leather seat next to Andre and crossed one leg over the other. "But we can only hold them off so long. When the ambassador doesn't show up for the meeting tomorrow morning, the media will be all over it."

"So how much time does that really buy us?" Andre's gaze remained on the screen.

"Since only our operatives know he's dead, we have until he doesn't show up in his room tonight."

"Why should that matter?"

"His wife will worry."

"Wait a minute. You guys didn't say anything about a wife." Andre leaned back in his chair and held up his hands.

Melody laid a hand on his arm. "Keep your shirt on, big guy. They're somewhat estranged."

"Somewhat?" Andre's eyebrows rose. "Define 'somewhat'."

"Insiders say they sleep in separate rooms and as far as anyone knows, they haven't made love in months."

Muscles knotting in his belly, Andre had a sudden feeling of being trapped. "You know how I feel about widows. I don't do widows. You can turn this plane around right now. I'm not doing it."

CALL ME BARBARIAN
Copyright © LIDDY MIDNIGHT, 2006.

"Oh, look! The gladiators are up next! You should hear the buzz among the women, about the two brothers from Sudania. They are quite the swordsmen, if you know what I mean." Her arch expression made me look at her a little more closely.

"Really?"

Before I could pursue this line of inquiry, fighters entered the arena and I became distracted, too busy admiring their oiled muscles and strutting bodies to start up a gossip session. As a rule, I understand, gladiators are a vain and rutting lot, but oh, are they gorgeous!

The southern brothers led the second round. From the moment they stepped forward, they dominated the arena. They moved with confidence and a charismatic quality that kept all eyes on them. Their peers and opponents paled in comparison. My pulse quickened and I could not tear my attention away, even when Tilda touched my elbow.

I could understand the excitement generated by their bouts in the ring, for they were in truly excellent shape. Not overdeveloped, as some bodies in the arena appear, but balanced and fluid in their movements. I admired their tanned skin and what looked to be strong profiles, although their faces were mostly hidden by their half-helmets.

Dark hair flowed down their backs, worn longer than is customary in the ring—especially as they favored trident and net as weapons. Those permit the wielder to capture his opponent's weapon and render it useless, then move in to grapple hand to hand. Close fighting can be dangerous with long hair, as it gives an opponent something to grip. Flexible as eels, the brothers eluded every attempt to hold them and won the ensuing wrestling matches in short order.

Flowers and coins showered into the arena as the crowd awarded them the victories. They had mastered what I call the "winning strut", the victory lap that every winner takes around the arena, to cheers and catcalls.

When they turned to acknowledge the Emperor and removed their helmets, my breath caught in my chest.

SPONTANEOUS COMBUSTION

"Tell me your deepest, darkest fantasies."

The words were breathed in a husky, sultry tone against Maddy's ear. Warm breath caressed her neck, raising the fine hairs at her nape and sending chills coursing down her spine.

She didn't have to turn around, knowing instantly to whom that deep sexy baritone voice belonged. How she would love to provide explicit graphic details of her most intimate fantasies for him. Or better yet, maybe they could act them out.

"Come on. Tell me, babe. What is it? Being bound to the bed, or maybe oiled up on a Slip N' Slide? Do you dream of sweet lovemaking, or hard fucking? One lover or several?"

Icy shivers prickled along her skin. Just the sound of his voice, his erotic words, had her nipples puckered and pressing against the bodice of her little black dress. She had worn it in hopes of catching his eye. Not that he would ever notice Maddy as a woman. His buddy, sure. A woman, never. His words were all in jest as usual, right?

"How much have you had to drink tonight, Jake?" she questioned, then gasped as he licked a hot wet path along the ultrasensitive skin behind her ear.

"Stop it, Jake!" Maddy squealed in protest. Of course, stopping him was the last thing she wanted to do. But giving in meant risking both heart and soul. She couldn't stand the thought of being rejected by this man, the only one who really mattered.

Jake Cruise had been her best friend and neighbor since college. They had shared everything. Well, almost everything. She couldn't share her true desires with him, could she? As if he'd ever want to have sex with her. He was such a tease.

Maddy gave herself a mental shake. What was she thinking? Of course she couldn't. It would ruin their friendship. Probably freak him out to hear her dark, forbidden passions.

DRAGONMAGIC

Arys felt his dragon body turn inside out, then there was a bright light and he was standing, naked, on two human legs inside a cozy, one-room cottage.

"Damn witch," he growled at the voluptuous woman bent over the fire. "What do you want now?"

The witch Clymenestra stood up calmly, eyeing him with her usual smugness. Arys was tall, with bronze-colored skin over hard muscle, waist-length white-blond hair, and dragon silver eyes. Clymenestra looked him over like she owned him.

The bitch knew his true name and could call him from Dragonspace anytime she liked. *Not forever, darling*, he thought. *Not forever.*

"I need dragon's blood," she said, letting her gaze rove his body.

"Always blood. What is your spell this time?"

"Never you mind." She looked at him with dark, possessive eyes. "I hold you, dragon, and you'll give me your blood." She smiled. "I'm always willing to pay for it."

He knew her thighs were wet with her cream, her opening hot, anticipating. Arys' cock was already swollen and hard, standing straight out from his body. His long hair warmed his back, but his arms prickled with cold in the night air. Human skin was too damn thin.

Clymenestra had bound him to her with the magic of his name—but one day, one day, he'd be free. He knew the secret of his freedom, she didn't.

"So you called me all the way from Dragonspace for a drop of blood?" he growled. "I was deep in important business."

"Two drops. And you were lying on your back in the snow, sunning yourself. Silver dragons are the laziest things in creation."

Arys didn't deny this. In his dragon form, he lived to eat and hoard and mate as often as possible. He also worked his own kind of magic, which was lightning fast, like a fiery needle in his brain.

He loved dragon magic. Human magic was too much like work.

FALLEN FOR YOU

"You think they'll try to kill me?"

"Yes." Zade wouldn't look at her. His gaze fixed on the streetlamp across from Isabel's bedroom window. The light's honey glow was a safer sight by far than the little witch drifting toward sleep behind him in the dark.

He was a Watcher, a once-mighty angel, and still this woman could bring him to his knees with a negligent sigh. Zade clenched his jaw, his hand fisting around the Roman coin he always carried in the pocket of his slacks.

Her soft, sleepy voice already had his cock as stiff as a Watcher's sword. And the scent of her sheath was only a wicked tease of how perfectly she'd fit his blade. His dick twitched at the thought, but he pushed the erotic image from his mind.

A rustle of covers, like the sound of a warm body rolling in bed, teased behind him. "Why now?" she said.

"Your skills have grown these past months. All those attuned to the ancient power will have felt your touch. You are a threat to the Oscurità as well as a temptation."

Her small snort was muffled in the pillows. "And here I was only hoping to tempt you."

Zade's nails dug into his palms, every muscle in his body coiling tight. He closed his eyes and reached soul deep for the strength to deny his need. He was here to ensure her safety and train her in the use of the ancient power—nothing more.

Isabel and her kind were the key to destroying the Oscurità, the prideful fallen angels. A mission he and his Watcher brothers had failed to achieve so long ago. For ten thousand years they'd suffered the punishment for their ill-fated complacency. Sentenced to an eternity linked in name and penalty with those they'd been sent to destroy.

She and her witch sisters were the Watcher's second chance and Zade would let nothing distract him this time.

THE JOINING
Copyright © JORY STRONG, 2006.

Rumors abounded of women not only being taken to brothels or sold as slaves, but of ending up on the nearby planet of Adjara, where the men formed marriages with each other, and needed a woman only long enough to produce a child for them.

Siria shivered. Little was known about Adjara. It was primarily a desert planet, harsh, unforgiving, closed to outsiders. Few in their right mind would attempt to go there, though the dream of gaining riches beyond measure by exploring the small range of mountains for rich deposits of precious stone had lured many to their deaths.

Her mother had been fascinated by Adjara, making it a game in the evenings to search though whatever news reports could be captured using their ancient computer. Telling Siria that her ability to locate water would make her a princess in such a place.

Once her mother had even found a rare picture of an Adjaran without the trademark robes and face covering they wore even when they weren't in the desert. He'd been stripped to the waist, his body bronzed by the sun, lean and fit from life on a planet where the weak didn't survive, one arm covered from shoulder to hand with exotic tattoos. Siria closed her eyes, remembering that day.

"Here's a prince to your princess," her mother teased.

"And what about the rumors of women being used to produce a child and then being disposed of?"

"I'm not so quick to believe them," her mother answered with a shrug. "Look at the rumors that abound on Qumaar!"

"You win. Of course, what makes the rumors about Qumaar so frightening is that the truth is often more horrifying!"

"True. Now admit he's handsome at least," her mother pressed, running her finger over the computer screen.

Siria knew when she was beat. "I'll admit it. He's handsome."

"And if rumor is true, he comes with a second man."

"Mother!" Siria yipped, her face flaming, only to realize by the play of expressions on her mother's face that she hadn't intended it to be a sexual comment. But once she did realize how her comment had been interpreted, her mother's laughter filled the room, contagious and fun, irresistible, and they'd both ended up in tears, holding sides that ached from their amusement.

"Still," Siria said, when they finally stopped. "No one has ever heard of a woman going to Adjara and leaving again."

Her mother shrugged. "The same could be said, except in reverse, for Qumaar. No one who leaves here is ever heard from again."

Enjoy the following excerpt from:
Nuworld - Thicker Than Water
By Lorie O'Clare
Book 6 in the Nuworld series.

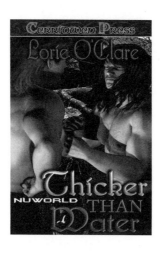

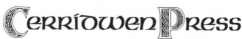

from

CerridwenPress

www.cerridwenpress.com

Mainstream eBooks

Titles for all tastes!

"Are you okay?" Ana sounded concerned.

"Yeah, I'm fine. I thought I would take the debriefings home with me if you don't mind. The children are anxious to see Andru, and I would like to be there as well. I can compile them there." She needed to get the subject off herself as quickly as possible. "So tell me about your trip to the south. I hear Bargstown is quite the booming community these days. Did you get to see Beel and Paleah?"

"We spent our second night with them. They have a beautiful home and Magi is growing like a weed." Ana smiled but then cocked her head at Meah.

"Your lip is swollen. Who got the better of you?" Her question was meant to tease and Meah tried to keep her expression light.

"I'm afraid I overdid it all the way around yesterday." She shrugged. "I'm sure I'll be fine tomorrow."

Ana seemed to accept the answer, but still studied her friend. "You wore your hair down for Andru. He loves it that way, although it certainly isn't too practical."

Before Meah could react, Ana had moved behind Meah and pulled her hair together. "I envy your straight hair sometimes. You can do so much with it. It feels just like Gilroy's hair but—"

Ana didn't finish and Meah turned around to face her. Ana looked worried, but when their eyes met, Meah didn't like what she saw.

"What is it?" Meah frowned.

"Someone bit you," Ana whispered.

"I'm okay." Meah gave the matter a wave of dismissal and returned to the landlink. "Over three-quarters of the debriefings are in," she added in hopes of changing the dangerous subject they bordered on.

"Someone attacked you, and I daresay you're protecting them. Why would you do that?"

"I'm not protecting anyone," Meah snapped, and turned around quickly.

"Okay, who bit you?"

"No one bit me. I must have been attacked by some bug or something." Her voice lingered. That was a mistake.

Didn't you vow never to lie?

"A bug or something." Ana's expression hardened, as she lifted Meah's hair and studied the mark on her nape. "This is no bug bite, and I'm no fool. You've been attacked. Give me the name now."

Meah stood so she was inches from Ana's face. The two women stared at each other for a long moment, before Meah sighed and looked down.

"I wasn't attacked...not the way you think," she whispered.

"Who did this?"

"Why does it matter?"

"It matters."

Meah looked up into those gray eyes. She licked her swollen lip and Ana watched the act.

"Gilroy," she whispered.

"Liar." Ana slapped Meah across the face and then backed away from her quickly. "How could you say that?"

"You shouldn't have asked." Meah's tone was barely audible as her hand went to her stinging cheek. "I don't ask you questions."

"What?" Ana whispered in disbelief.

Meah fought to suppress a fury that churned deep within her. She had to remember her place. This conversation bordered on insubordination and her temper would push her over the edge. She breathed in deeply then exhaled in an attempt to stifle her anger. The progress of the debriefings seemed to move at a snail's pace.

"Don't turn your back to me. How can you say you weren't attacked?" Ana made no attempt to stifle her anger. "How many more marks are on you? Look how stiffly you're moving. I'm no fool, Meah."

"You're no fool?" Meah spun around, forgetting the lecture she'd given herself seconds ago. "You sleep with Andru again and again. You bear his children and you think your claim idly sits around and ignores this?"

Ana moved in quickly and shoved Meah against the landlink. Meah fought to maintain her balance and turned a furious glare on her leader. Ana's gray eyes were black with outrage.

"Who the hell do you think you are to talk to me like that?" She spat the words.

"I don't want to fight with you. Drop it, Ana."

"No. I want you to tell me. Tell me exactly what you're saying."

"I'm saying Gilroy made these marks on me."

Ana raised her hand to strike again, but this time Meah blocked it. The two women stared at each other venomously.

"He raped you."

"No." Meah shook her head.

Ana pushed herself away from Meah and backed up a step or two. She ran her hands through her braided hair and a curled strand fell over her face. She brushed it away with contempt and studied Meah for a long minute.

Once again, Meah fought to get her emotions under control. She turned her back to Ana and watched the screen until it showed all debriefings were in. Pushing several keys on the keypad, the landlink began humming as it transferred the debriefings to the disc. Her hands shook and she held one in the other as she ordered herself to calm down. There was a chilling silence in the trailer, and she could feel Ana's icy stare on her back.

Ana strolled over to stand next to Meah. She continued to stare at her first commander. Unable to stand it any longer, Meah turned her head to meet her leader's gaze.

"How often does Gilroy come to you?"

Meah shook her head. "Don't ask me these questions. I don't ask you how many times Andru comes to you?"

"That's different."

"Is it? Do you think Gilroy and I don't feel the pain of our claims sleeping together? What about Darien? What about your firstborn child?"

Ana shook her head adamantly. "Tell me you were raped, Meah. Tell me, and I'll handle it."

"What are you going to do? Have your claim flogged?" Meah stared at Ana and she worked to make sure she said the right words. "No, I don't think so. Ana, I wasn't raped."

"Then you seduced him."

Meah looked at her in disbelief. How could she tell her what her claim did to her? What they had done together? How could she tell her without giving her more pain than the woman was already experiencing? She wouldn't be able to bear Ana describing her times with Andru. But this whole conversation stemmed from a lie. She told herself it probably would have come about had she told the truth from the start, although it was no consolation. She wouldn't lie about this.

"I think you went after Gilroy. You did it before. You wanted him, and you forced yourself on him because you can't handle sharing Andru. You have no choice and you're too damned stubborn to accept the fact that you can't control everyone. I bet Gilroy taught you a lesson and you're afraid to admit it."

"You know that's not true!" Meah screamed the words as she lunged at Ana. Her rage consumed her so quickly that she didn't think—she just acted. She drove into Ana with a force strong enough to send her leader toppling backwards.

The two women fell over the chair behind Ana and sprawled to the floor. Meah fell on top of Ana and her body screamed from the inflictions that already existed. The pain stunned her long enough for Ana to slide out from underneath her, but Meah moved to a squatting position quickly.

Ana pounded Meah squarely in the jaw with her fist. The iron taste of blood filled Meah's mouth, but she wasn't daunted. She flew from the ground and leaped on Ana again, raising her hand quickly to retaliate. She wasn't thinking. Her actions turned to pure instinct, calling out the warrior in her. She'd been attacked and she prepared to return the action. Her mind was so consumed with the harsh words that berated her soul—the inaccuracy of them.

Meah didn't hear the door open, and she didn't notice the movement behind her. A large gloved hand wrapped around her neck and propelled her backwards. She literally flew across the room and fell into a small table next to the couch. She slid off it and crumpled into the corner, her legs awkwardly sticking up in the air around the destroyed table.

"Don't you ever lay a hand on my sister!" Andru screamed the words at her and she looked up, momentarily confused and disoriented.

Meah struggled to get up, but her bruised body, now inflicted with even more pain, refused to cooperate with any ease. She pulled her legs down from the side of the table and they fell loudly to the floor. She wiped her hand across her face, smearing blood, and shoved hair from her face simultaneously. Andru reached down and grabbed her before she could regain her footing. He lifted her and she saw blind fury in his eyes. Panic flooded through her.

"Andru, I didn't want—"

He threw her onto the couch as she swallowed her words. Meah stared blankly up at him and then slowly tried to rise to her feet. Ana moved to her brother and grabbed his arm. He pulled away from her quickly, and Gilroy, who stood silently behind him, moved a step to the side to avoid his leader's hasty movement.

Ana balled her hands into fists and turned her fury on her claim. "She's been bitten on the back of her neck. Did you do this to her?"

He didn't answer. Meah brushed her hair out of her face, and twisted it into a ball while she stared at the ground. The silence screamed at her. Gilroy didn't want to hurt Ana any more than she did.

"I hate you," Ana hissed, and Andru grabbed her arm.

She yanked her arm away as Meah looked up. Gilroy blocked her path and she pushed both of her hands full force into his chest.

"Get out of my way," Ana hissed, and then stormed out of the trailer.

Meah felt uncontrollable tremors consume her and sank backwards into the couch. She grimaced, and adjusted herself involuntarily as pain raked through her. It took all her inner strength to sneak a glance at her claim. His hands were in his hair and he stared at the ground.

"What did you say to her?" The words were thick with outrage.

Her hand shook as she covered the side of her mouth and she spoke slowly. "She saw the mark on my neck that you saw. I didn't know it was there, Andru. I didn't mean to cause her any pain." Tears fell without obstruction down her cheeks.

Andru focused on her and then simply stared for a moment. He finished running his hands through his hair and then turned to leave. "I'm going to my sister. You two have debriefings to deal with."

Meah jumped when the door slammed shut. She moved slowly to stand, and Gilroy was across the room in an instant to help her.

"I'm okay." She waved him off.

"Like hell you are."

She moved to the landlink and extracted the disc then shoved it into her pocket. She didn't look at Gilroy when she turned around but instead took in the broken furniture in the room. What a mess! And simply cleaning up the broken furniture wouldn't fix things this time. Gilroy followed her silently out the door.

He threw his leg over his glider, but made no attempt to start it. Instead he leaned forward and relaxed against the handle bars as he watched Meah put her hands on her own handle bars and then attempt to climb on. She didn't get too far. He stifled a grin as she gritted her teeth and lifted her leg again. Gilroy got off his glider and was behind her when she failed to mount her glider the second time.

He placed one arm gently around her shoulders and the other arm went down behind her knees. She fell into him willingly and he lifted her with ease onto her glider.

"What do you want to wager that within the hour the only title I'll possess is the claim to the Lord of Gothman?" Meah situated herself on her glider to where she felt the least amount of pain.

"We won't let that happen, my lady," he spoke quietly, and stroked her hair away from her face.

"Gilroy," she complained, looking quickly around the tree-shaded area to see if anyone was watching.

"I'll follow you home," was all he said, as he backed away from her to his own glider.

Why an electronic book?

We live in the Information Age—an exciting time in the history of human civilization, in which technology rules supreme and continues to progress in leaps and bounds every minute of every day. For a multitude of reasons, more and more avid literary fans are opting to purchase e-books instead of paper books. The question from those not yet initiated into the world of electronic reading is simply: *Why?*

1. ***Price.*** An electronic title at Ellora's Cave Publishing and Cerridwen Press runs anywhere from 40% to 75% less than the cover price of the exact same title in paperback format. Why? Basic mathematics and cost. It is less expensive to publish an e-book (no paper and printing, no warehousing and shipping) than it is to publish a paperback, so the savings are passed along to the consumer.

2. ***Space.*** Running out of room in your house for your books? That is one worry you will never have with electronic books. For a low one-time c ost, you can purchase a handheld device specifically designed for e-reading. Many e-readers have large, convenient screens for viewing. Better yet, hundreds of titles can be stored within your new library—on a single microchip. There are a variety of e-readers from different manufacturers. You can also read e-books on your PC or laptop computer. (Please note that Ellora's Cave does not endorse any specific brands. You can check our websites at www.ellorascave.com or

www.cerridwenpress.com for information we make available to new consumers.)

3. *Mobility.* Because your new e-library consists of only a microchip within a small, easily transportable e-reader, your entire cache of books can be taken with you wherever you go.

4. *Personal Viewing Preferences.* Are the words you are currently reading too small? Too large? Too... ANNOYING? Paperback books cannot be modified according to personal preferences, but e-books can.

5. *Instant Gratification.* Is it the middle of the night and all the bookstores near you are closed? Are you tired of waiting days, sometimes weeks, for bookstores to ship the novels you bought? Ellora's Cave Publishing sells instantaneous downloads twenty-four hours a day, seven days a week, every day of the year. Our webstore is never closed. Our e-book delivery system is 100% automated, meaning your order is filled as soon as you pay for it.

Those are a few of the top reasons why electronic books are replacing paperbacks for many avid readers.

As always, Ellora's Cave and Cerridwen Press welcome your questions and comments. We invite you to email us at Comments@ellorascave.com or write to us directly at Ellora's Cave Publishing Inc., 1056 Home Avenue, Akron, OH 44310-3502.

Discover for yourself why readers can't get enough of
the multiple award-winning publisher

Ellora's Cave.

Whether you prefer e-books or paperbacks,

be sure to visit EC on the web at
www.ellorascave.com

for an erotic reading experience that will leave you
breathless.